HEAD OVER WHEELS

ROAD TRIPPING SERIES

SAMANTHA CHASE

HEAD OVER
Wheels

Cover Design: Uplifting Designs/Alyssa Garcia

Editing: Jillian Rivera Editing

PRAISE FOR SAMANTHA CHASE

"If you can't get enough of stories that get inside your heart and soul and stay there long after you've read the last page, then Samantha Chase is for you!"

-*NY Times & USA Today Bestselling Author* **Melanie Shawn**

"A fun, flirty, sweet romance filled with romance and character growth and a perfect happily ever after."

-*NY Times & USA Today Bestselling Author* **Carly Phillips**

"Samantha Chase writes my kind of happily ever after!"

NY Times & USA Today Bestselling Author **Erin Nicholas**

"The openness between the lovers is refreshing, and their interactions are a balanced blend of sweet and spice. The planets may not have aligned, but the elements of this winning romance are definitely in sync."

- **Publishers Weekly, STARRED review**

"A true romantic delight, *A Sky Full of Stars* is one of the top gems of romance this year."

- **Night Owl Reviews, TOP PICK**

"Great writing, a winsome ensemble, and the perfect blend of heart and sass."

"Well? What do you think?"

Danielle Perry had overseen the restoration of dozens of classic cars since coming to work for Malcolm and Son Restoration, but this was the first time the sight of a finished car brought tears to her eyes.

This one was personal.

She had felt a connection to this car from the beginning that had her feeling overly emotional, and she was *not* an emotional person.

Ever.

Staring down at the black and white photograph in her hand, she blinked away the tears.

"Dani?"

Beside her stood Malcolm and son. Well, Malcolm Sr. and Malcolm Jr., such as they were.

Malcolm Sr. had started his classic car restoration business back in the nineties. The man lived, breathed, ate, and slept classic cars, so it was no wonder he passed his love of all things automotive on to his son.

Looking up, she met Malcolm Jr.'s eyes and felt herself blush.

Averting her eyes quickly, she cleared her throat. She looked at the photo and then back up at the car before saying, "It's perfect." The next time she looked up at father and son, she saw the look of relief on both of their faces. "Seriously, you guys outdid yourselves. This car is...well... it's a dream."

Malcolm Sr. smiled broadly before coming to stand beside her. Wrapping an arm around her shoulders, he hugged her. "Don't sound so surprised," he teased.

"I'm not!" she replied, stepping away, her eyes wide. A nervous laugh was out before she could stop it. "I'm just..." She paused and collected her thoughts. "It's like part of this photo has come to life."

Both men nodded.

The truth was, it was simply a coincidence that the 1960 Corvette convertible was the same one from the photo in her hands. Her grandparents and great-grandparents were in the photo; her grandfather purchased the car back in 1962 to soup it up for the sake of racing it. He never got it onto a track, but the picture was a snapshot in time where everyone was young and carefree and enjoying the possibilities of a great car. Her old, Italian great-grandparents were in the front seat wearing sunglasses and giant smiles.

It was a great photo.

It was a great car.

And if she didn't get her head out of her butt, it was going to be the reason she turned into a blubbering mess.

Straightening, she cleared her throat. "Okay, are you ready to go over the checklist?"

Malcolm Sr. groaned and took a step back. "That's my cue to leave. Good luck!"

Dani didn't think it was possible for a man his age to sprint—especially one who complained about his knees on a daily basis—but he practically left them in a cloud of dust. Shaking her head, she laughed softly. Glancing at Malcolm Jr., she smiled.

There wasn't anything she wanted more than a chance to be alone with him and this trip was finally her chance. There wasn't a thing about him that didn't attract her—from his tall, muscular build, his jet-black hair, baby blue eyes, and arms covered in tats. Add in the fact that he was a genuinely nice guy who was a little on the quiet side, and he was practically catnip for her.

For three years she had been pining for him and it hadn't gotten her anywhere. It didn't matter how hard she flirted or tried to impress him with her knowledge of classic cars; he just never took the bait.

Or maybe he just wasn't interested.

Nope. Not gonna go there. I'm sticking with him being clueless.

But if she could be alone with him outside of the garage, maybe things would be different.

It wasn't like he was completely indifferent to her. He was always bringing her stuff from his trips to deliver their cars—mostly tacky things from souvenir shops because he knew she loved that crap. It was really kind of sweet how he always did that. She had three shelves filled with plastic snow globes, shot glasses, candles, assorted figurines, and gifts from him in her apartment and they always made her go all soft and dreamy.

"You okay, Dani?"

"Uh...yeah. Why?"

He shrugged. "You sort of zoned out there. We were going to go over the checklist?"

"Oh. Right." *Way to go, dork.* Looking down at the tablet in her hand, she swiped the screen and pulled up the necessary information. "Is the car completely secured?" Right now it was chained to the flatbed truck she and Malcolm would be driving from the shop in Raleigh, North Carolina, down to Jacksonville, Florida, with a few stops along the way.

Nodding, he said, "Check."

"Do you have all the final documentation for the car— registration, insurance, title?"

Frowning, Malcolm looked at her. "Wait, isn't that in your folder along with directions, our reservations, our registration to the show, and all that? Maybe I should be the one going over the checklist and making sure you have everything."

She knew he was joking, but...

Handing him the tablet, Dani hung her head. "That makes more sense. All you needed to do was secure the car to the flatbed. Everything else was on me so..."

The low snort he let out was his only response.

Sighing dramatically, she said, "Okay, fine, you spent three months and hundreds of hours restoring the car from a broken down, rusted-out piece of junk to a shiny showpiece. There. Happy?"

His slow grin had her practically standing in a puddle of her own drool.

He looked down at the tablet and frowned. "There's an awful lot of stuff on here."

"There was an awful lot of stuff to do," she replied sweetly—secretly enjoying his reaction to all the things she had to handle for him.

Clearing his throat, he said, "Let's take it from the top. Final documentation?"

"Check."

"Hotel reservations?"

Doing her best not to smile, she nodded. "Check."

"Registration packet for the Concourse Classic Car Expo?"

Another nod. "Check."

"GPS programmed?"

"It's all done," she finally said. "Trust me. Plus, I've packed up a cooler with drinks, Reese's Pieces, Cheetos, Oreos, and some grapes. You know, in case you wanted to eat like an adult."

He laughed softly. "Thanks."

"My pleasure." Looking around, she caught a glimpse of the last thing that needed to be done. "All that's left is for you to put our luggage in the truck and we'll be ready to go!"

With a curt nod, he handed her the tablet and walked away.

A soft, dreamy sigh was out when he bent over to pick up their bags. Malcolm had a fine butt—especially in faded denim. She was going to have to make sure she didn't do that while they were on this trip. No need to freak Malcolm out.

Although...she had a feeling it was going to happen no matter what because they had never spent this much time in such close proximity. And she was planning to use that to her full advantage.

For the life of him, Malcolm had no idea how he was supposed to handle being alone with Dani for five days.

Well, five days if everything went according to plan.

And with Danielle, that rarely happened.

She had a knack for taking something simple and making it complicated–usually in the name of making things better–but he was a man who enjoyed having a plan and sticking to it.

"One of us may not survive this," he muttered.

"Survive what?"

Turning, he saw his father walking toward him, and rather than answer him, Malcolm finished stuffing the luggage behind the seats.

With little more than a groan, he turned around. "Are we sure this is the right thing to do–asking Dani to go on this trip with me?"

"Why? Don't you?"

He shrugged. "I don't know. I just don't want this to drag out and you know how she can be..."

His father snickered. "And you know she gets results. Our business changed for the better when we hired her, and this little project will only help solidify our name. She's a real people person."

"I guess."

"Wait, you're not nervous about traveling with her, are you?"

"Well..."

"Because if you ask me, it's going to be a good thing for you."

"Me?" he cried. "Why?"

"Malcolm, you're a good man. A fine man. But you move at a damn snail's pace and it's painful to sit back and watch."

Straightening, he stared at his father as if he'd lost his mind.

Malcolm Sr. continued, "Dani is a beautiful woman

who looks at you like you hung the moon and if you don't get up off your ass and show her some attention, some other guy will. How would you like that?"

"Did you hit your head today or something?" he asked incredulously. "Dani's had quite a few boyfriends since she's worked here. Why would her dating someone bother me?"

The look his father gave him in response told him just how little he believed him. The truth was, it would kill him if Dani found someone and got serious with him, but...that didn't mean he was the right guy for her either. He didn't have the best dating record. So much of his time and energy was spent working and he knew he could get consumed with a restoration. More than once he'd been dumped simply because he seemed to care more about the cars than the girls.

He didn't want to do that to Dani. She deserved better.

"Think about it." And with a huff of annoyance, Malcolm's father walked away.

Damn. Raking a hand through his hair, Malcolm let out a long breath. He hated how well his father knew him and hated even more that he was in this position. The last thing he wanted to do was disappoint Dani—not only because he genuinely cared about her, but because she really was an important part of the business. He thought he was doing the right thing by not pursuing her—the business always had to come first—but was he really doing the right thing?

It took him less than a second to answer that. Of course he was doing the right thing. Hadn't he watched his old man ruin three marriages because of his obsession with cars? And wasn't he following right in his footsteps? It was in his blood—his love of working on cars and bringing them back to life! When he wasn't working on a car, he was thinking about the cars he hoped to restore or going to car shows to see the work other classic car enthusiasts had done. As much as it meant he didn't have much of a social life–or a private one–he was content.

Well...mostly content.

"Hey," Dani said with a smile as she approached. "You ready to hit the road?" She looked so excited and hopeful and...beautiful. Dark hair pulled up into a ponytail, big green eyes, and the pinkest, glossiest lips he'd ever seen.

He was starting to sweat.

"Uh, yeah." Raking a hand through his hair, Malcolm knew he couldn't procrastinate any longer. They had a schedule to keep. Stepping aside, he opened the passenger door for her and watched as she climbed up. Today Dani had on a pair of black skinny jeans and a snug pastel pink t-shirt.

I'm not going to survive this...

Once she was settled, he slammed the door shut and walked around to the driver's side like he was walking to his own execution. On his way around, he double-checked the Corvette and made sure it was secure, and when he climbed into the cab, he stopped and froze.

"How long was I out there?" he cried, looking around in horror. Snacks were littering the center console and drinks in every available cup holder. Dani's shoes were off, her feet were resting on the dashboard, and she was singing along to some awful pop song on the radio.

"Oh, sorry," she said sheepishly, reaching out to lower the volume. "When you didn't climb in right away, I thought I had a few minutes with Taylor."

"Taylor?"

She nodded, smiling. "Taylor Swift. That's who was just singing. I love that song."

"Yeah, can't say I'm a fan," he murmured, buckling himself in. "I guess we should talk about rules."

"Rules?" Her smile faded. "Seriously?"

"Dad and I normally do these things together and... quietly." Hell, he couldn't even force himself to look at her.

"Ooohhh," she said after a minute. "Got it. Sorry." Bending forward, she reached into her oversized purse and pulled out a pair of earbuds. "No worries. I'll keep my music to myself. And I promise not to be too much of a bother."

"That's not what I meant..."

"No, no, no...I get it," she said right before making a zipping motion over her lips and popping her earbuds in. He was about to put the truck in reverse when she pulled the buds out and twisted to face him. "Malcolm?"

"Hmm?"

"Thank you."

He frowned. "For what?"

"For trusting me to help you with this. I think this trip is going to be a good thing for us." She paused and blushed. "I mean...for the business. It's going to be a good thing for the business." And before he could comment, the earbuds were back in and she was settled in her seat, humming softly.

Yeah, I'm not going to survive this...

2

"When we stop for lunch, can I take over driving?" she asked hopefully.

"Hell no."

Eyes wide, mouth agog, she stared at him. "Excuse me?"

The damn man never took his eyes off the road. "You can't drive the truck, Dani."

"Why not?"

Somehow, Malcolm even managed to make condescension look sexy.

"Seriously? You're a terrible driver! You can barely handle driving your car without getting into trouble. There's no way you can handle the flatbed," he reasoned. "And considering we're hauling a car worth one hundred thousand dollars, I'm unwilling to take that risk."

Well that was a little harsh...

With a huff, she sat back in her seat and stared out the side window. Damn the man and his honesty. What did he think would happen if she drove the truck on the interstate for an hour? How much damage could she actually do? Crossing her arms over her chest, she pouted. She knew she was pouting, and if Malcolm turned his head or even glanced at her, he'd see it, but she didn't care. She was pissed and he should know it.

Not even a minute passed before she huffed, "I don't see what the big deal is. I would totally respect the car and the truck. I'm not an idiot." She snorted before mumbling, "I *really* don't see what the big deal is."

And that's when Dani heard something she never heard before.

Beside her, Malcolm mimicked her sound—snorting with annoyance.

Turning, she looked at him. "What was that?"

"What was what?"

"That snort! What have you got to snort about?" she demanded. If there was one thing she had learned about Malcolm in the last several years, it was how he hated confrontation of any kind. Well, with anyone except his father. The two of them had had some major blowups in the garage, but if anyone else pushed, he tended to back down.

"Just let it go, Dani. You're not driving. Period."

"Then I want to go home," she said, resuming her pouting position.

"I'm not taking you home," he said mildly, reaching for the radio and turning it on.

She reached out and turned it off. "Then when we stop for gas or for a break, I'll just call my mom or someone to come pick me up."

"We're not scheduled to stop for another two hours. You can't expect your mother to drive that far to come get you." Again, his tone was completely calm and reasonable and it just irked her that much more.

"My mother would drive anywhere to get me if I needed her," she countered, feeling slightly smug.

"But you *don't* need her, Dani. You're just being a brat because you're not getting your way."

It didn't matter that he was completely accurate, but it pissed her off how well he knew her.

"I bet your father would have let me drive," she murmured.

"I'm sure he would have," Malcolm agreed, as if he didn't have a care in the world. "And then regretted it. But he's not here so..."

In that moment, she knew it was pointless to keep arguing. The man was as stubborn as he was honest, and this wasn't a fight she was going to win.

At least not now.

So she turned the radio back on—the classic rock station Malcolm favored—and forced herself to relax and think of something else to talk about.

"You've been to this car show before, right?"

Nodding, he replied, "We used to go every year. The last few years we've been too busy to do it. This is the first time we've entered a car of our own into the show. Usually we just go to see what's out there."

"And you're really going to sell it at the auction?"

"Yup."

Unable to help herself, she sighed.

Malcolm briefly turned his head to look at her. "What's wrong?"

"It's nothing," she said but knew she was lying. "If I had that kind of money, I would have bought the car myself."

"Because of the photo?"

"Yeah. I know it's crazy because it's not the actual car, but...I don't know, ever since I was a kid, I've loved those pictures. There's a whole series of them with both my grandparents and great-grandparents. I even have one framed in my apartment. Everything about them was cool and now that I've seen the car in person..." She trailed off, knowing she sounded ridiculous. It was an unattainable dream—not to mention unrealistic. As Malcolm already said, she was a terrible driver. There was no way she should even consider owning a car like that. There was no doubt that she'd ruin it in a heartbeat.

"You okay?"

Turning, she glanced at him. "I'll be fine. I don't know why I'm being like this over a car." She shook her head. "It's weird, right?"

"You think everything's weird," he countered.

That surprised her. "I do not!" she cried. "When have I ever said that things feel weird?"

He glanced her way again. "You really want to do this?"

"Yeah, I really do. Let's hear it."

Shifting slightly in the driver's seat, he rested one arm on the door and the other on the steering wheel. "You think it's weird how I don't drink coffee."

"Everyone drinks coffee!" she argued with a small laugh. "Ever see the lines at Starbucks?"

"Clearly not."

"Okay, fine. What else have you got?"

"You think it's weird that my father never took me to Disney World."

"Again, everyone's gone at least once, Malcolm. People travel from other countries to go there."

He shrugged. "I don't see the appeal."

With a dramatic sigh, she said, "In having fun? Uh, yeah. I got that. Go on."

"You've commented numerous times how you think people who haven't binge-watched *The Office*, *The Hand-*

maid's *Tale, The Walking Dead*, and *Game of Thrones* are weird."

"They're great shows!"

"You openly mock people who can't name all the...wait, who are they? The Kardashians?"

"Everyone knows them, Malcolm! And it's not hard to remember, all their names start with K's!"

"You also mock people who don't stay up to date with celebrity gossip and pop culture or who don't watch TMZ."

She was beginning to see a pattern here...

"And you think it's weird that people do!" she countered. "So I'm not the only one who has issues or thinks things are weird."

Another shrug. "I never said you were. I'm just saying that *you* think everything is weird and not just a few random things."

"You know, I could point out all your issues too."

"I'm sure you could," he said with a low laugh. It was low and gruff and when he turned his head and smiled at her, she felt herself tingle from head to toe.

Dammit.

"But unlike you, I happen to find all of your quirks...endearing."

"Endearing?" He didn't sound like he believed her even a little bit.

Nodding, she said, "Uh-huh."

"Now this I've got to hear. No one's *ever* called me endearing."

Well...shit. Was he really going to make her explain? But when she didn't expand–simply because she was too embarrassed–Malcolm reached over and gently patted her on the knee while smiling.

"That's what I thought," he said, but not before his

hand casually skimmed a little higher before he pulled it away.

In that moment, Dani began to wonder if this attraction really was all one-sided.

"Dani?"

"Hmm?"

"Do you mind telling me why we only have one room instead of two?" They were riding up in the hotel elevator in Hilton Head and he was surprised she wasn't freaking out about their accommodations.

"Your dad's always going on about not spending too much money, so I just followed all the travel arrangements you've used in the past. I didn't think it was a big deal."

"Well, this is a little different. Do you want me to get you your own room?" he asked, hoping he sounded casual about it because he was nervous as hell about sharing a room with her. The front desk clerk said it was a king room with a sleeper sofa, so at least they weren't sharing a bed. "I don't mind taking the sleeper. You can have the bed."

He looked over and saw her chewing on her bottom lip–something he wouldn't mind doing–and waited for her to respond.

"I mean...I guess it's not a big deal." She looked up at him with a nervous smile. "But I can take the couch. You're a big guy and I'm sure you'd be way more comfortable in the bed."

Of course he would, but he still was going to be a gentleman. "I'm fine on the couch. Trust me. You take the bed."

She studied him for a moment and he wanted to look

away, but he couldn't. She looked just as nervous as he did and that was at least some consolation. "If you're sure..."

The elevator arrived on their floor and they silently made their way to their room.

"Malcolm?

Nodding, he opened the door to the room and followed her inside. "I'm sure." He looked around and there was plenty of room for the two of them with a small living room, a desk, the bed, and a bathroom. It wasn't ideal, but it also wouldn't be a hardship to spend the night there together. "What do you say we freshen up and then go grab some dinner? The restaurant downstairs looked nice or we can see what else is in the area."

But Dani shook her head. "Ugh, the last thing I want to do is get back in the truck. I'm ready to walk around and stay put for the night."

"It wasn't that bad..."

"Trust me, I love a good road trip, but I'm just ready to walk and not drive."

"I hear ya," he murmured, taking in his surroundings. Walking over to the closet, he spotted the bedding he'd need. Behind him, he heard moving around.

Staying where he was, he watched her check out the space before sitting on the bed and bouncing on it slightly. She looked at him and grinned. "Ooh...memory foam. My favorite."

Great. Just what he needed—not only knowing the kind of bed she preferred but also seeing her bounce on it.

Clearing his throat, he turned, picked up his bag, walked over to the sofa and opened it up. It was a queen size, but it was still going to feel small and cramped for him. Not that he was going to say anything to Dani about it. Silently, he went to work putting the sheets and blanket on it and once that was done, he went into the bathroom and washed up. When he stepped back out a few minutes later, Dani excused herself to do the same. With nothing left to do, he called down to the front desk to see if they would need reservations for dinner and reserved a table for two for one hour.

He had no idea how long Dani would need to get ready, but he didn't want to rush her. They had driven a lot of miles today. They had stopped in Myrtle Beach to meet with a classic car collector who was mildly interested in the Vette before driving on to Hilton Head for the night. Taking some time to sit and relax was something he was completely on board with.

With nothing else to do, he got comfortable on his bed and turned on the TV. After channel surfing for several minutes, Dani stepped out of the bedroom and smiled at him.

"Whatcha doing?"

Shrugging, he motioned to the television. "Just seeing if anything's on. I called and made our reservations for dinner downstairs at seven. I hope that's okay."

"It sounds perfect," she said sweetly as she sat herself down on the edge of his bed.

Without thinking, Malcolm moved over to give her more room, and before he knew it, she was practically lying down with him. He didn't say a word but as he normally did when she got too close, he felt himself starting to sweat.

"Mmm...this bed's comfy too," she said, her voice soft and a little sleepy. "Do you think there's time for a quick nap?"

"Um...I guess," he stammered. "I could call and move the reservation to later or we could just get room service if you'd prefer."

Beside him, she lifted her head. "Would you prefer to get room service?"

If we could eat it in bed naked...

Forcing that thought aside, he forced himself to keep his focus on the TV. "I thought it would be nice to go down and eat. I figured you'd like it."

"Aww...you are so sweet," she cooed. "I really don't need a nap. This was just super comfortable. I'd like to go downstairs too. It's not every day I get to go out to a fancy restaurant. It will be like a date!" Then she rested her head back down on the pillow and got comfortable again.

Say what now? A date? Uh...

"Oh, I love this show," she said, interrupting his thoughts. "I always try to figure out which house the couple is going to buy, but somehow they never pick the one I think they should." Shaking her head, she added, "I wish they'd all just listen to me."

Unable to help himself, he laughed. Leave it to Dani to think her way was the only way.

"I'm telling you," she went on, "I have great taste in houses and what kind of space will work best. If I wasn't working for you and your father, I'd totally be kicking ass in real estate."

"Dani, I have a feeling you'd kick ass in anything you did," he murmured.

Beside him, she lifted her head again, her expression a little soft and...happy. "Malcolm King, that may be the sweetest thing you've ever said to me."

Was it possible he was blushing? He could swear his cheeks were heating up.

"What?" he said, hating how gruff he sounded. "You know we think you do a great job with everything you do."

Her expression fell slightly before she nodded. "I know.

You and your dad are always praising me and I appreciate it. I'm glad you're both impressed with my work."

Had he said something wrong?

Before he could ask, she was back in her position again with her head on the pillow. "Come on. Let's see what their options are. Then you tell me which house you think they should pick and I'll let you know if I agree. We already missed the first two choices, but they'll recap them at the end before they decide."

It was a harmless game to play and he figured it would kill some time before they went down to dinner. And he had to admit, she made some valid points as she talked about each house. Once the episode ended, another one started so he got to watch it with her from the beginning.

They laughed, they argued, and by the end of the episode, the couple chose the house neither he nor Dani picked and he understood her frustration.

She jumped off the bed and stretched. "Give me two minutes to grab my shoes and purse and I'll be ready to go!" He watched her walk away and began to second-guess his decision to skip out on room-service. They had been having such a good time that he hated to interrupt it.

But he had nothing to worry about. They continued to talk about the show all the way down to the restaurant, and once they were seated, the conversation switched over to favorite foods and places to eat. The menu was full of Italian food–something he already knew Dani loved–but he found he enjoyed listening to her talk about her favorites and why certain meals held special memories of her family.

Once the topic of food was exhausted, she asked about the next car he was going to work on and that turned to a long conversation about cars. He'd never dated a woman who showed any interest in what he did beyond how the car looked. Dani had a working knowledge of what went into a full restoration and he enjoyed knowing that she understood everything he talked about.

Before he knew it, they had finished their dinners and dessert, it was after ten and the restaurant was closing. They both apologized for staying so long and laughed softly as they made their way out of the restaurant.

"I am so full," she said, her hand on her flat stomach as they waited for the elevator. He had to hand it to her; she didn't shy away from food. If anything, she ate almost as much as he did—and that was saying something.

"I don't think I should have had the second slice of cheesecake," he replied. "But damn, it was good."

"Cheesecake totally isn't my thing, but that Death by Chocolate cake was literally to die for."

The elevator arrived and they stepped inside. They rode up to the room in companionable silence and he hated how the night was coming to an end. He opened the door to their room and let her go in first and wondered what they were supposed to do now. Would Dani go right to bed? Were they going to talk? Watch TV? Personally, he enjoyed staying up late and watching the television until he fell asleep, but...that was him.

Without a word, she stepped into the bathroom and shut the door.

Huh...that's kind of rude...

Shrugging, he walked over and grabbed his suitcase and was suddenly glad he'd packed some sweatpants to sleep in. Within minutes, he was shirtless and back on his bed flipping on the TV.

Then he heard the bathroom door open.

Dani walked out wearing a pair of black leggings and an

oversized Malcolm and Son t-shirt. She made herself comfortable next to him. "What are we watching?"

I seriously wish this woman came with a manual...

He shifted over to put some distance between them without being obvious. "Um...I haven't found anything yet. I was thinking one of the late-night talk shows."

"Is that what you usually watch?" she asked around a loud yawn.

"Sometimes."

Turning her head, she looked up at him and Malcolm noticed she didn't have on a stitch of makeup and, if anything, she looked even more beautiful than she normally did. "Well, what *would* you be watching if you were home?"

Shrugging, he replied, "I don't know. I kind of just channel surf until something catches my attention. But we can probably find another one of those home shows if you want."

"Mmm..." she hummed. "Okay."

Within minutes, they were settled in and casually commenting about the pros and cons of the home that was currently being featured. When the show went to a commercial, Dani turned to him again. "Malcolm?"

"Hmm?"

"I had a really great time tonight."

Smiling, he said, "Me too." He could tell she had something else to say, so he waited her out.

"I want you to know, I realize this wasn't like...you know...a real date, but it was the best date I've had in a long time." Then she sat up a little straighter and kissed him softly on the cheek. "I think I'm going to crawl into my bed. I'll see you in the morning."

Right then and there, he knew he wasn't going get a wink of sleep.

3

"Do you want to grab breakfast down in the coffee shop or should we just hit a drive-thru on our way out of town?" she asked as she zipped up her suitcase the next morning.

"Uh..." he cleared his throat and she could tell he was a little uncomfortable.

Good.

She was glad she wasn't alone.

Mortification kept Dani burrowed under her blankets until she heard Malcolm go into the shower this morning. She hadn't slept more than a couple of hours all night because she had been kicking herself for her behavior last night.

The only problem was that she couldn't decide which she was more upset about—the fact that she had all but crawled into bed with Malcolm without being invited and then kissed him, or the fact that she had been a complete wuss and chastely kissed him on the cheek instead of doing what she really wanted to do.

"Who am I kidding? I'm pissed I didn't straddle him

and kiss him until he couldn't remember his own name," she mumbled beneath her breath.

"You say something?"

With a small screech, she jumped. Hand over her heart, she turned and faced him. "Geez, Mal! Don't do that!"

He looked at her like she was crazy. "Do what? Talk to you?"

"Ha, ha, very funny." Grabbing her suitcase, she carried it over to the door before walking around and making sure they hadn't forgotten anything. When it was clear they had everything, Dani smiled at him. "So...breakfast. You know I'm not a big breakfast person, but if you're hungry, we should probably eat before we hit the road."

"Uh...yeah," he finally said. "Sure. Sounds good."

He wouldn't look directly at her and once they were in the elevator with several other hotel guests and standing close together—very close together—she could feel how stiffly he was standing. She took advantage of the opportunity to study him. His jaw was stubbled and scratchy and she wouldn't have minded kissing him again and lingering there all morning if given the opportunity.

Down in the lobby, he announced that a drive-thru was just fine and quickly made his way out the front door. Chuckling to herself, she took care of checking out before meeting him out by the truck. She found him examining the car and making sure the tarp over it was secured.

"It's a gorgeous day, don't you think?"

He nodded.

"We have an eleven o'clock appointment with Devlin Bennett in Savannah. It's only an hour away so there's really no rush, right? Maybe we can do a little sightseeing before we have to meet him?" she suggested.

Without looking away from what he was doing, he said,

"I'm not much for sightseeing." He didn't sound angry or annoyed; he was simply stating a fact.

Typical Malcolm. Nothing seemed to ruffle him.

A slow smile spread across her face as an idea came to her. Maybe it was time to push some boundaries, leave her own comfort zone, and see if it was possible to...ruffle him.

And boy-oh-boy would she love to ruffle him.

Repeatedly.

For hours.

Down, girl...

"What about...?" But she never got to finish. Malcolm grabbed their luggage and placed it in the truck and held the door open for her to climb in. Before he could close it, she kicked her foot out to stop him. "Hey," she said softly.

He looked up at her questioningly.

"We've still got quite a few days to get through together. Any chance you can relax a bit?"

Brows furrowed, he said, "What are you talking about? I'm relaxed."

"Mal, you've barely talked to me all morning and now we've got an hour of driving to kill. I'd rather not spend it with my earbuds in again. Please." She gave him a sweet smile in hopes of softening him up, but...

"We need to get going," he murmured, closing the door.

Once he was settled in behind the wheel and they were on their way, Dani pulled out her phone and began doing some searches. After they had gone through the drive-thru of McDonald's, she figured she'd start the conversation.

"Do you want me to sit in on this meeting with Mr. Bennett? Is his place anywhere near the historic district? Because if you don't need me with you, I thought I'd do one of those trolley tours. There are some seriously cool ghost tours, but I'm guessing those are done at night. Do you think they're done at night? I'm sure they're better when it's dark out."

"Dani?"

"Hmm?"

"It's too early for all those questions. Maybe ask one and wait for me to actually answer it."

She laughed softly. "Yeah, I know I tend to be too chatty in the mornings. Sorry. Normally I'm in the office starting my day and you're in the garage under a car. I'm usually on the phone talking to people so...I'll keep quiet until you've finished your breakfast. How does that sound?" If she didn't have sunglasses on, he'd see she was batting her lashes at him.

With nothing more than a grunt and nod, Malcolm resumed eating his breakfast biscuit while driving. It was on the tip of her tongue to offer to drive but she knew that would get her nowhere. They had made such strides last night over dinner and it bothered her that he was back to his quiet ways today.

What to do...what to do...

Now that she had gotten a glimpse of how funny and sweet and charming he could be outside of the garage, there was no way she was going to settle for going back. They still had almost a week away together. Tomorrow was going to kick off the hardest and busiest time for them with the auto show, and she refused to spend it acting like they were just co-workers or casual acquaintances.

But for right now, she had to bide her time and not push too hard.

So she would wait for him to finish his breakfast and his coffee, then give him some time to simply relax and then...

Then she was going to do her damnedest to bring out the man she had finally seen last night.

Something was up.

They had finished their appointment and lunch with Devlin and were back on the road. She hadn't gone on the trolley tour or any haunted ones–something he never would have pegged her for–and something just felt...off. Dani came to the appointment with him to discuss a restoration on a 1969 Dodge Charger. She had sat in on consultations at their shop, but this was the first time she came to meet with a client. He figured she'd sit back and maybe just observe, but she didn't. Instead, she joined in the conversation and offered some great insight into the process Devlin was looking to schedule with him.

Malcolm always knew Dani had a strong working knowledge of what went into the restoration of a classic car, but he found himself beyond impressed with the way she handled herself.

And a little uneasy at the way she handled *him*.

First it was a simple hand on his forearm. Honestly, he didn't think anything of it. But then she touched his bicep–all the while talking to Devlin–and squeezed.

Twice.

By the end of the conversation, her hand was resting on his thigh and he had no idea how he was going to stand up without it being incredibly awkward–and obvious–how much her touch affected him.

She did the same thing to him over lunch, but luckily, he had the table for protection.

It was like he was thirteen again and being asked by the teacher to show his work up on the board while dealing with an unexpected erection.

So yeah, something was definitely up and Malcolm was finding it hard to believe it was all because of last night.

Although last night was...incredible. He couldn't remember the last time he'd gone out for a meal with a woman and enjoyed himself more. Then back at the room, for those few minutes when she was beside him in bed, he felt like everything was exactly as it should be. He felt peaceful and happy and...then he wasn't. Looking back, he never should have let her simply kiss him on the cheek and then leave. He should have hauled her into his arms and kissed her like he'd been fantasizing about for years.

Years.

What kind of man waited that long without going after what he wanted?

A stupid one...

Yeah. That.

The problem was...okay, *one* of the problems was that the business was doing really well right now. His father had spent years barely breaking even and then making enough of a profit to live comfortably. They were finally in a place where they were both making good money–great money. And Dani was one of the reasons that finally happened. She had come in and taken over their marketing, handling all communications with their clients, and then created their social media accounts – something neither him or his father had a clue about. She had a knack for it and the results of her efforts came in fast. They could barely keep up with the demand for restorations. Their waiting list was eighteen months long! Did he really want to mess that up by starting something with her when he knew he was going to mess it up?

Way to be confident, dude.

It was hard to argue with his track record.

There was no way he wanted Dani to be included in his disastrous dating history. She didn't deserve that. But he also didn't want to jeopardize their working relationship. Maybe she wouldn't mind seeing him every day after things went south, but he'd feel like shit if he had to walk in and look at her beautiful face and know that he'd screwed up.

Then let this go...

Easier said than done.

Right now, she was sitting beside him quietly—her earbuds in—and smiling as she listened to music so she wouldn't distract him. He shook his head with disgust. She was only doing it because he had all but snapped at her earlier about how chatty she was. He kind of felt like crap about it because she had only been trying to make conversation.

Before he could second-guess himself, he reached over and tapped Dani on the shoulder. Her smile was sweet and instantaneous.

"What's up?"

"So, uh...I was wondering, uh...I mean...I just thought um..."

If she had any attraction to him, there was no doubt that it was dying a slow, painful death, he thought, unable to believe how tongue-tied she made him.

Her eyes went a little wide but her smile never wavered.

"You don't need to sit with those things in your ears," he said gruffly. "We can talk...you know...if you want."

I loathe myself...

"I didn't want to bother you," she replied sweetly. "It seems to me you prefer it to be quiet when you're driving."

Normally he did, but...maybe it was time to try something different. "Who's your favorite band?" he asked, offering her a small smile.

After that, it was like they both relaxed back into the people they were the night before. Malcolm couldn't even help himself. She drew things out of him he didn't normally talk about–like growing up working on cars and how hard his parents' divorce was on him. The divorce was something he never talked about, and yet with Dani...it felt completely natural.

"Do you see your mom a lot?" she asked. "I don't think I've ever heard you talk about her in all the years I've worked for you."

"She lives in Nashville now and she's always on me to come visit, but...I usually only go once a year."

"How come?"

He shrugged. "There just never seems to be a good time to go. We've got so much going on with the shop and Dad's...I don't know if you've noticed, but he's slowing down a bit. I hate leaving everything on him so I can go play tourist with my mom."

"Hmm..."

Turning his head slightly, he looked at her. "Hmm, what?"

"I guess you sided with your dad then," she commented. "You know, in the divorce."

"Not really. Why would you think that?"

Now it was her turn to shrug. "I don't know. It just seems like you're completely settled in with him and he's your priority. Not your mom."

Huh. He never really thought of it like that.

"It's not like I purposely chose sides," he explained. "I've always enjoyed working on cars and it's something Dad and I always did together. When they split up, I had to divide my time living with the two of them. Mom was still living in Raleigh at the time, so I stayed with her during the week and with Dad on the weekends. She moved and remarried after I graduated high school."

"Do you like your stepfather?"

Did he? "Uh...yeah. Steve's a cool guy and he takes good care of my mom." He paused. "She deserves that. My father always put cars and the business first. It's why he's been married three times. So when she met Steve, it was...it was a little eye-opening."

"In what way?"

"She...she blossomed," he said and realized how stupid he sounded. "Or...I don't know. Something like that."

"No," she said, resting her hand on his denim-clad thigh. "I know what you're saying. She suddenly seemed happier, right?"

Nodding, he said, "She laughed more and I swear she suddenly looked...younger. I don't know. I started to feel like whenever I was around, I was a reminder of the crappy life she used to have."

"Malcolm, you can't look at it like that! Oh, my goodness! Why would you even think that? Did she ever make you feel that way?"

"No," he said firmly, and he meant it. "She's always thrilled to see me and makes a big fuss over me, but...I guess it's how I feel. I feel like an outsider when I'm there."

She was quiet for a moment. "Okay, I'm going to say something and please don't take offense."

"O-kay..."

"Do you think you feel that way because of your own feelings? Like...you see the life she has now and you resent it because it's not the life you got to have growing up?"

Well damn. Now he did!

"I never thought of it like that. My folks divorced when I was ten, and even when they were together, it was never...

it was never like it is with her and Steve. They do things together, he works a normal job, they have friends they go out and socialize with, they travel…"

"All the things she never did with you and your dad."

"Exactly."

"You know you're following in his same path, right?" she asked, and he could hear the hesitation–the uncertainty–in her voice.

All he could do was nod.

"I'm not trying to be mean and maybe I'm speaking completely out of turn, but…"

"You're not, Dani. Trust me. I see it happening and yet…I can't seem to stop it." They fell silent for several moments and he was thankful for it. "I love what I do and I'm good at it. And I think this is the way Dad's done things for so long he doesn't know how to change."

Beside him, she twisted in her seat so she could face him. "Malcolm, it doesn't matter if your father changes. It's not all about him. This is about you. If you're not happy with your life, you're the only one who can change it. Have you guys ever thought about hiring more people? I know you subcontract some of the body work out, but…what about just having a couple more guys on hand to help out?"

"It's an expense to hire more people and I'm not sure…"

"You've got a long waiting list of clients and if you had a few more guys working for you, you'd get more cars in and out faster. It's just something to think about."

"I know."

After that, Dani talked more about the benefits of hiring a couple of guys and he chimed in when he had something to say, and he felt like a giant weight had been lifted off of him. He never talked to any of his friends about his discontent or the ways he wished the business would grow and change and he realized it was something he should have done sooner because...he needed to.

His father had started the business, but he was a partner in it now and he should have a say in how things went. Just because they had done things a certain way for so long didn't mean they always had to do it that way.

As a matter of fact, just because he had been doing things–like avoiding Dani–for so long, didn't mean he always had to.

And when they got to the hotel, he was done avoiding.

4

THE HOTEL WAS similar to the one from the night before

They were staying in a suite.

They had gone out to dinner, and as they headed back up to the room, Dani had butterflies in her belly.

Tonight she wasn't going to settle for kissing Malcolm on the cheek.

Tonight she was going to be brave and take what she wanted.

And man oh man did she want Malcolm.

Being in such close proximity to him all day for two days had her on sensory overload. She could smell his cologne, study every feature on his face, listen to him talk and laugh...but mostly, she watched his hands.

And fantasized way too hard about how they were going to feel on her skin.

Yeah, tonight was the night.

Malcolm opened the door to the room and once they stepped inside, she considered her options. Did she go change like she did last night or did she stay out here with him? Hmm...

"I have something for you," he said gruffly, breaking into her thoughts.

"You do?" She smiled up at him and hoped she didn't sound as giddy as she felt.

Nodding, he walked across the room and opened his suitcase, pulling out a small plastic bag. Dani moved in close. He turned and handed it to her. "I saw it earlier when we checked in and knew you'd like it."

Gah...did he have any idea how much she loved when he did stuff like this?

Peeking into the bag, she could feel her smile growing to almost painful proportions. Inside was a palm-sized stuffed animal–a pug. She had talked a lot over the last several years about her family's pet pug, Penelope, and how she wanted a pug puppy of her own someday.

"I know it's not a real puppy," he said, his voice low and so damn seductive, "but when I saw it, I knew you needed it."

Looking up at him, she felt tears sting her eyes. "She's perfect," Dani said quietly. "Thank you."

Here's your moment...

Gently placing the toy and bag on the table, she moved in close to him. "That was incredibly sweet of you."

Malcolm's gaze was intense, and if anything, it made her bold.

Carefully, she placed her hands on his chest and slowly moved them up and over his shoulders as she pressed in closer. "Very, very sweet of you," she whispered before she closed the distance between them and pressed her lips to his.

She was prepared for him to be shocked.

She was prepared for him to maybe kiss her back briefly and then move away.

But there was no way she was prepared for the total onslaught of sensations as Malcolm reached up and anchored one of those wonderfully large hands in her hair and took over the kiss.

Holy. Crap.

There was no easing into it; it went from lips touching to all-consuming in the blink of an eye and Dani did her best to keep up. The man kissed with the same intensity he did everything and she was more than happy to be on the receiving end of it. His tongue stroked hers in the most erotic way. Her head spinning, and she was more than anxious to move things from where they were standing in the living room to any surface they could lie down on.

Reaching up, she raked her hands up into his hair right before she broke the kiss and nudged his lips to her throat.

And damn did it feel good.

"Malcolm?" she said breathlessly. "The couch. The bed. Anyplace but..."

She was up and in his arms before she even knew it and was pleasantly surprised when he placed her down on the bed. As much as she wanted to take a moment and catch her breath, Malcolm was still a flight risk and she wasn't ready for this to end. Her hands fisted in his hair as she pulled him in close.

And she happily sighed with relief when he lay down on top of her and settled between her thighs.

Best. Night. Ever.

The kiss went on and on, and as much as she was enjoying it, Dani desperately wanted Malcolm to touch her. Everywhere.

As if reading her mind, his hands began to move—caressing her cheek, cupping her breast, before snaking under her shirt and undoing her bra.

Yeah, I could die right now and be completely happy...

And just like her fantasies, the rough skin of his hands felt incredible–panty-melting. And the more he touched, the more places she wanted to be touched. She squirmed underneath him, all but humping his thigh to get some friction and relief where she wanted it most.

Clearly the man took hints well because no sooner had her actions become a little frantic when his hand reached down and cupped her between her thighs. He lifted his head and gave her the sexiest smile she had ever seen.

"Is this what you want?" he murmured against her lips.

"Yes," she sighed. "For starters."

His husky laugh made her all tingly–or maybe it was his hands–but either way, she was so close to having an orgasm that she was almost embarrassed. She'd never come this fast from foreplay, but she wasn't going to complain. And no sooner was that thought out of her mind than she felt like she was soaring. Dani clutched for him even as she panted his name over and over and over. And when she finally settled down and felt completely boneless, all she could do was look up at Malcolm and say, "Wow."

One dark brow arched at her. "You okay?"

"More than. Please tell me we can do more of that."

"Dani..."

And that's when she heard the hesitation in his voice and knew she had to think and act fast.

"Just tonight, Mal. Please." She knew she was lying because one night was never going to be enough. And she prayed if she could just get him to let down his guard for this one night, she could get him to change his mind about them.

About a future.

He sat up, straddling her, and pulled his t-shirt up and

over his head, and she almost wept with relief. They had this one night for now, and she was going to try her hardest to make it one he'd want to experience again and again.

"As you can see, we went with the two-tone exterior, pairing Roman Red with Ermine White in the sculpted side panels," Dani was saying the next day. They were setting up for the auto show and the Corvette had already drawn a lot of attention. Normally his father was with him and handled talking to enthusiasts if he was busy, but right now Dani was holding her own.

She moved to the front of the car, placing her hand on the hood. "The hood has a front hinge and you can see the three-unit front grille."

She looked like a denim-clad Vanna White—but instead of turning over letter tiles, she was walking around the car and motioning to every detail she talked about.

"We restored the original dual headlights in the front fender," she went on before walking around to the driver's side of the car and motioning to the handle. "Push-button door handles and key locks. And as you can see, we went with the soft folding top with the power-operating mechanism for safe and easy folding." She looked over at him with a shy smile before she continued with her spiel.

It was hard to say which turned him on more—the fact that she was the perfect combination of sweet and sexy or that she knew so damn much about cars.

Then the image of bending her over the car and having his way with her like he had last night came to mind and he realized he didn't have to choose between the two.

They equally turned him on and in this particular scenario, it was like he could have his cake and eat it too.

The images that statement brought to mind had him ready to...

"So are you looking to sell or are you just showing it?"

Snapping out of his reverie, Malcolm forced himself to put his attention where it needed to be and spent the rest of the day talking about the Vette. The show hadn't even officially started–this was just the day to set up–and he already wished it was all over. The only thing keeping him sane was the fact that he and Dani were heading back up to the room.

Last night, he swore it was only going to be a one-time thing.

Well, three times, but only the one night.

It was amazing no one could smell smoke, because surely his pants were on fire for that lie.

They walked across the lobby and into the first elevator along with about ten other people. They were packed in tight but he still noticed as Dani leaned against the back wall, sighing. "Oh, my gosh. I don't know how you and your dad do this sort of thing all the time. It's exhausting!"

He laughed softly, mimicking her pose. "And we haven't even started yet. Car enthusiasts love to talk. If you think today was exhausting, tomorrow's going to double it." Beside him, he saw her pout. "What's the matter?"

"So you're saying we've got three more days of...all that and more, right?"

He nodded.

"And I should probably rest as much as I can so I can handle it, right?"

Another nod.

"Well," she glanced around and frowned. "Son of a mother trucker."

"Uh...what?"

She nodded toward the family with a young boy standing in front of them and he realized she didn't want to curse in front–or behind–them.

Which was kind of cute.

But also made no sense. "I don't get it," he said after a moment.

Rolling her eyes, Dani sighed with relief when the doors slid open on their floor. She stepped out and was walking five paces ahead of him, leaving him more confused than ever.

Was she mad at him? Was she sorry she came on this trip and wished she could go home?

He was just about to offer to leave a day early because she was clearly unhappy. But as they walked into the room, she turned and gave him a shove. Malcolm's back hit the wall as the door slammed shut. "What the..."

And then she was in his arms and climbing up him like she was more than a little crazed.

And he loved it.

They clumsily made their way over to the bed, knocking over the luggage rack, banging into the dresser, and tripping over a pair of Dani's shoes–but all the bruises he was going to have were worth it as he laid her down. As he settled on top of her, she wrapped herself even tighter around him–which he didn't think was possible.

Kissing her was something he was coming to crave.

Touching her was practically a religious experience.

And hearing her soft purrs and moans were the most erotic sounds ever.

Everything in him told him not to let this go any further, but there was no way he could stop now–not after knowing how good they were together. Maybe tomorrow he'd see things more clearly. For all he knew, this was just a matter of the two of them scratching an itch or simply giving in to curiosity or even just a way to pass the time.

Liar...

Hell, it didn't matter what he thought because in another minute, he wasn't going to be able to think of anything except how much he hated his own stupid thoughts.

So he shut his brain off and let his body take the wheel.

5

"CAN I DRIVE THE CAR?"

"What?!" Malcolm's head snapped around so fast that Dani was surprised he didn't break it.

Smiling sweetly, she placed her hand on his arm. "Oh, come on...the show's over and I know we're hitting the road in the morning. Can't I just take it for a spin around the parking lot? Please! The back lot is huge and most of the cars are gone so it will totally be safe! I love this car so much and it's just for sentimental reasons. I'd love to tell my grandpa how I drove one just like his."

Her eyes welled with tears and she knew she was laying it on thick, but for a good reason.

"Dani..."

"Please, Mal!" she begged. "I'll be careful, I swear!" It was no secret that she was a lousy driver–or how random things seemed to get in her path, forcing her to dent and scratch her car–but how much trouble could she get into in an empty parking lot?

"Um..."

Moving in close, she clutched the front of his shirt. "I'm begging you. This would mean so much to me!"

She knew in that instant that she had him. His shoulders sagged and he let out a long breath. "We're supposed to deliver the car to the buyer, Dani. It's not my car anymore."

"No papers have been signed," she said and immediately held up a hand when he went to argue. "And nothing's going to happen. Just five minutes around the parking lot, Mal. Then we'll load it onto the flatbed and be on our way. I swear."

Malcolm took a step back and muttered a curse. Raking both hands through his hair, he stared hard at her. "Don't make me regret this..."

"Yay!" Hugging him, Dani placed a loud, smacking kiss on his cheek. "Okay, let me grab my purse and..."

"No," he quickly interrupted. "In the morning. It's already getting dark out and I want you to have full visibility when you're driving."

"That's a little insulting..."

"No, the way you think you can drive is insulting," he countered before letting out another long breath. "Just... please. Can we do this in the morning?"

"Just as long as you promise not to change your mind."

His smile was slow and a bit lopsided but utterly adorable and instead of answering her, Malcolm took her by the hand and led her across the event space, back through the hotel lobby, and up to their room.

Good to know he's not changing his mind about us, either...

Yeah, she had to admit, she really expected him to stick to the initial one-night thing, but this was going on to night three and she certainly wasn't going to be the one to rock the boat. So she followed along, loving how big and strong his hand felt wrapped around hers. Inside she was doing cartwheels and skipping around with unicorns.

God, I'm such a dork...

Once they were back in their room, she turned to ask him about dinner, but–for the first time–Malcolm was the one to initiate the contact. Dani was seriously beginning to wonder if he ever would and he did not disappoint. His big, work-roughened hands cupped her face as he dove in for a kiss that was all heat and need and a little dirty. It didn't take long for her to go from "oh my" to "take me now."

And it was so glorious that all thoughts of dinner and cars were completely forgotten in a flurry of clothes flying and limbs tangling.

She had no idea how much time had passed but by the time she was staring up at the ceiling as she tried to catch her breath, Dani was fairly certain she'd died and gone to heaven.

Greatest trip ever...

And as she curled up next to Malcolm with her hand gently resting on his chest, she couldn't help but smile.

"Mal?"

"Hmm?"

"Thank you," she said softly.

His low chuckle was his first response. "My pleasure."

Men...

"Not for what we just did–although it was spectacular–but I meant for this trip. For trusting me enough to bring me along. It's been amazing." Pausing, she pushed herself up so she could see his face. "I've wanted something to happen between you and me for so long and...and I just want you to know how much you mean to me."

It was a little dim in the room, but she could have sworn he looked mildly uncomfortable.

Maybe I just rocked his world a little too hard...
Sure it wasn't realistic, but for now, it was all she had.

"I thought you said you knew how to drive a stick!" Malcolm yelled the next morning as he all but yanked Dani from the car.

"No, I said I know how to *ride* one," she said saucily with a wink.

"Dammit, Dani, this isn't a joke! Not only did you nearly grind the transmission out of the damn car, but you jumped the curb!"

"There was a squirrel!" she cried. "He was eating a bagel! What was I supposed to do, hit him?"

Pinching the bridge of his nose, Malcolm silently counted to ten. "Just...get in the truck," he said, his voice low and menacing. There was no way he could even look at her right now. She'd look at him with those big green eyes and he'd crumble. And right now, that wasn't what needed to happen. He'd spent months working on this car–getting it into prime condition–and she'd nearly wrecked it all because of a bagel-eating squirrel.

And the thing that pissed him off the most was that he knew better. He knew she couldn't even drive an automatic car without getting into trouble. What had possessed him to think she'd be able to handle the Vette?

Obviously he was thinking with the wrong head and that was *not* acceptable. How would it look if she had done real damage to the car? How would he possibly explain that to the buyer? It was the kind of thing that could ruin the reputation of the business he and his father had been building for years.

What the hell am I doing?

Off in the distance, he heard the truck door slam and knew things were going to have to be dealt with. He hated confrontation and unfortunately, that's what was going to happen once he joined Dani in the truck. But before he could even think about it, he needed to inspect the car and see what kind of damage she did and then get it up on the flatbed.

There were some scuffs on the front passenger tire and some dirt, but luckily that was all. Then he got behind the wheel and drove it around the parking lot a couple of times to make sure the transmission was okay. Once he felt confident that it was, he went through the process of getting it loaded and secured. By the time he climbed into the truck, almost an hour had passed. Dani was pouting and wouldn't even look at him, and right now that suited him just fine. They had seven and a half hours of drive time to get through and he seriously wouldn't mind starting it out quietly.

"I can't believe you're pissed at me," Dani stated with a huff.

So much for the quiet...

"You conveniently forgot to mention that you don't know how to drive a stick shift, Dani," he said calmly. "That car is going to sell for close to a hundred thousand dollars. It's not a damn toy!"

And feeling less calm by the minute.

"I mean, did you even think about that?" he demanded. "Did it even cross your mind how you could do serious damage to the car?"

"Well..."

"And honestly, I don't appreciate you playing me like that!"

"Playing you? Are you for real right now?"

Nodding, he glanced at her as they pulled onto the interstate. "Yup." Honestly, he couldn't remember ever being angrier. He just wasn't sure if it was Dani he was mad at or himself.

This show was a big deal.

This car and the sale of it were big deals.

And he'd almost ruined it all because he couldn't say no to Dani.

Well that's going to change...

Malcolm expected a fight—Dani never shied away from one—but this time, she did. Without a word, she pulled her earbuds out, tucked them in her ears, and began fiddling with her phone. It wasn't until they were crossing the state line between Georgia and South Carolina that she spoke.

"Can we stop and grab something for lunch?" she asked, almost defiantly. "I know you're anxious to get back to the shop, but I'm hungry. If you don't want to stop, I'll just wait and grab something when we stop for gas."

It was on the tip of his tongue to argue that he wasn't trying to starve her or torture her, but he kept it to himself. Instead, he said, "No problem."

Lunch was painfully quiet and so was the remainder of the trip. When they arrived back in Raleigh, she grabbed her luggage and tossed it into her car before he had a chance to put an end to this. Reaching out, he gently grasped her arm and spun her around.

"What?!" she snapped. All signs of the meek and quiet woman he drove with for almost eight hours were gone.

"Okay, this has gone on long enough," he said with all the heat he could muster after such a long day. "I'm not going to apologize for being pissed, Dani! What you did was irresponsible, and you know what? I'm equally mad at myself!"

"Because you think I played you?" And yeah, that was total sarcasm.

"Oh, please, you know that's what you did! Looking up at me with those sad eyes and giving me the story about wanting to share the experience with your grandfather..." Pausing, he rolled his eyes. "You've asked to drive the car before and I've always said no! And apparently, with good reason!"

"The squirrel was eating a bagel! How many times do I have to...?"

"I don't care about the squirrel! I care about how the car is a game changer for the business! I'm going to have to come in early tomorrow and get it up on the lift to make sure there isn't anything wrong—no scratches or dings or dents from your little test drive!"

"There's not going to be any damage, Mal," she countered. "It wasn't a very high curb. And you know what? It was worth it. I've been wanting to drive that car since it came in and I'm glad I finally got the chance, even if it pisses you off."

And that's when it hit him.

"Is that why you did it?"

"Did what?"

"Slept with me?"

Her eyes went wide as she took a step back as if he'd slapped her. And then she spun away and climbed into her car, speeding away and spewing gravel in her wake.

And jumping the curb because a pigeon was in the middle of the driveway.

Go figure.

6

"Oh, Dani girl. What did you do now?"

It was early on a Sunday morning, a week after she and Malcolm had gotten back from the car show, and she walked into the office to find his father. She knew he always came in on Sundays to pay bills and it was the perfect time to get him to look at her car.

And the most recent damage.

"Those trash cans weren't supposed to be there," she murmured. "Can you change out the taillight for me? Please? I don't want to get a ticket."

"You don't want my son to see, either," he teased, rising from his chair. "Otherwise you would have waited until tomorrow to show this to me."

"Yeah, yeah, yeah...I guess." Together they walked out to the parking lot where she showed him the damage to the rear bumper. "I keep telling Mr. Mateo not to leave his pails so close to my driveway..."

Malcolm Sr. simply patted her on the shoulder before squatting down to look at her car. "Broken taillight, scratches on the bumper, and it looks like your rear quarter panel took a hit too." Straightening, he glanced over at her. "You know I can't fix all of this today."

"I already bought the taillight. Can you switch it out for me and then we can talk about the rest? I can live with the scratches." Her shoulders sagged. "We both know there's no point in fixing them because there will only be more soon."

Nodding, he placed an arm around her and led her back into his office. Once he had her seated, he leaned against his desk. "Want to talk about it?"

She looked at him oddly. "We just did. I hit the trash cans."

"That's not what I meant and I think you know it. I'm talking about you and my son. I heard about your spin with the Corvette."

Unable to help herself, she hung her head, too embarrassed to look at him. "I really screwed up. I was so focused on wanting to drive the car that I didn't really think about how it not only wasn't a good idea, but how I didn't know how to drive it." She sighed. "Now Malcolm's not talking to me—won't even look at me—and..."

"Can I let you in on a little secret?"

She nodded.

"My son is overly cautious and needs to unclench."

Okay, that was surprising.

Well, not exactly surprising—she'd been saying the same thing about him for years. It was just surprising to hear his own father say it.

"He seems to think the Corvette is some sort of game changer for us, but it's not. Don't get me wrong, it drew a lot of attention, but our business was doing fine before it and it's going to continue to do fine once the new owner shows up to pick it up."

Looking up at him, she frowned. "But I messed it up!

That's why it's still here, right? There was more damage to it than Malcolm actually thought and it's all my fault! That can't look good for you guys–to have to delay delivery. Even I know that."

"Dani..."

"Just...whatever the cost of all the repairs, you can deduct them from my paycheck. Maybe not all in the same paycheck...you know...a little at a time until it's all paid off, but...I am more than willing to pay for the damage."

His smile was almost serene and seemed oddly out of place considering this conversation.

"Dani, there was no extra damage to the car other than a small scuff. The car is still here because the owner has been delayed. So please stop worrying."

So the car was fine and still Malcolm wouldn't talk to her.

And that spoke volumes.

She would have confronted him about it already, but he had gone out of town on Thursday to look at a 1967 Ford Mustang up in Virginia.

Convenient...

"Listen, Malcolm," she said glumly. "I've been thinking..."

"Oh, no," he quickly interrupted. "I already know what you're going to say, and whatever it is that happened between you and my son is none of my business, but I'm not going to let it affect us working together. We're all adults and just...just give him time, Dani. Trust me. It's going to get better."

Tears stung her eyes as she looked up at him. "I just don't know if I can stay on working with him. It's too hard. It's only been a week and it's been so awkward."

"He's been gone most of the week."

"And when he calls in, he calls you on your cell rather than calling the office like he always did. Trust me, it's not going to get any better."

Reaching out, he pulled her to her feet and hugged her. "I'm sorry you feel that way, but I'm telling you, be patient, okay?"

The old guy had never let her down and she hated to disappoint him, so...she supposed she could stick it out for a little while longer.

Taking a step back, she turned to grab her purse, tripped over her own foot and stumbled into the chair before knocking it on its side.

Malcolm Sr. immediately helped her to her feet as he chuckled softly. "Pretty soon we're going to have to wrap you in bubble wrap for your own protection."

Sadly, it wasn't the worst idea.

I'm a jerk.

I'm such a moron.

If I could, I'd kick my own ass.

Yeah, this was pretty much Malcolm's mantra since Dani had literally spewed gravel in his face a little more than a week ago. He was miserable. Even looking at her hurt and from the look on her face whenever he would sneak a peek, he could see she looked just as unhappy as he was.

Not the finest example of misery loves company, but there it was.

As he parked his truck next to the Malcolm and Son garage, he stared at the bag on the seat beside him and prayed it was enough to make things right.

Or at least better because right now, things sucked.

Honestly, they'd sucked for a long time—long before he and Dani went to the car show together. After spending some long sleepless nights since coming home, he realized he wasn't happy with his life. He wanted more.

He wanted Dani.

There was going to be a lot of crow to eat and he had a feeling she was going to make him grovel way more than he was comfortable with, but whatever it took, he was up for. Spending his life living and breathing nothing but cars and this business was slowly killing him. It was time for him to learn from his father's mistakes and forge his own path.

With a steadying breath, he climbed from the truck, bag in hand, and walked into the garage. He was feeling more than a little apprehensive because this could all blow up in his face. Maybe he waited too long or had been that big of an ass and Dani wasn't going to forgive him.

Or maybe he had misread their time together completely.

Totally not the option he was going with...

Pulling open the side door to the garage, he stepped inside and immediately spotted his father bent over the engine of a '77 Trans Am. He lifted his head slightly and wished him a good morning before putting all of his attention back on the car.

Without breaking stride, Malcolm walked through the garage and up to the front where Dani's work area was. She caught sight of him with a soft gasp right as she knocked her coffee cup and a stack of files onto the floor.

The woman was the biggest klutz he had ever met and it was one of her most endearing qualities.

Dropping the bag on her desk, he quickly grabbed some paper towels and helped her clean up the coffee spill before the files got ruined.

But not before they banged heads when they both bent down to pick them up.

Dani muttered a colorful string of curses and he did his best not to laugh.

And failed.

"What the hell, Mal?" she demanded as she stood back up.

"What? I was helping you clean up! I didn't think it was a big deal."

He knew the instant she realized he had a point. Not that it helped. If anything, she looked ready to strangle him. So for his own safety, he stepped around to the other side of the desk and picked up the bag he had brought in with him.

"Here," he said. "I got you something while I was up in Virginia."

All she did was blink at him before turning and going to get herself another cup of coffee.

It wasn't quite the response he was hoping for but he could wait her out.

All day if he had to.

Several minutes later, she was back and gave him a bored look. "Still here?"

Smiling, he said, "I've got nothing else to do." Then he held out the bag again. "Come on, Dani. Open it. Please."

She carefully placed her mug on her desk, a safe distance away from the edge, and begrudgingly took the bag from him. Reaching inside, she pulled out what he'd gotten her. After she stared at it, she held it up and glared at him. "Seriously? You got me a *Virginia is for Lovers* key chain? What is wrong with you?"

Malcolm wanted nothing more than to move in close and hold her, but he had to bide his time for a little longer. "There are actually a lot of things wrong with me, Dani, and the main thing is that I miss you." He held his breath and waited for a response but didn't get one. "I'm so sorry for the way I reacted back in Jacksonville and that whole damn day. If I could go back and change it, I would."

Still nothing.

"Believe it or not, I had a great time with you on that trip. You opened my eyes to all the things I've been missing in my life. You've always been here for me—every day you are the one bright spot in my life. I look forward to coming to work just so I can see your face and hear you laugh and just talk with you. And then when things changed...well...I didn't think what we had could get any better, but it did."

Now he did move in close and was relieved when she didn't back away.

"You are everything to me, Dani. I know I can never take back the things I said or the way I acted, but if you'll give me a chance to make it up to you well, I'd really like the chance to see where this goes with us You're it for me. I think I knew that a long time ago but I was too scared to take a chance."

His arms went around her waist and she softened a little against him.

"Danielle Perry, I am head over heels in love with you. Tell me I didn't ruin everything. Tell me I'm not alone in how I'm feeling."

She looked at the key chain in her hand and then up at him. "You're not the only one who needs to apologize, Mal. I was a brat and I never should have tried to drive the Vette. I should have just asked you to take my picture in it so I could show it to my grandpa. He would have gotten a kick out of that too. I'm sorry I put you in an awkward position and I've been kicking myself about it for a week. I missed talking to you every day and I missed just seeing your face."

And...he wanted to prompt her.

"And you're not alone," she said, her cheeks going an adorable shade of pink. "I've been in love with you for so damn long but never thought you'd feel the same way about me. That road trip was like an answer to a prayer. I knew if I could get you out of this shop..."

He never let her finish.

Claiming her lips with his, he felt her melt against him as she gave as good as she was getting. If his father wasn't out in the garage, he would lay her down on the desk and do some of the things he'd fantasized about over the last few years.

But there would be plenty of time for that later.

When they finally broke apart, he caressed her cheek and smiled down at her. "There's a reason I chose a key chain for you."

"Oh, really?"

Nodding, he kissed her forehead. "I was thinking of switching out the transmission in the Vette and modifying it to an automatic one so...you could drive it."

Pulling back, she looked at him as if he was crazy. "Mal, you can't do that! The new owner wanted it restored to its original state!"

"Yeah, well, I was thinking of canceling the deal with him and...keeping the car. For you."

She stepped back and stumbled over her chair and clumsily fell into it. "Are you crazy?! You can't just back out of a deal like that! The car is worth a fortune! It's going to be a huge boost to the business!"

"Dani..."

"No, I'm serious, Mal! I need a car that's made by Fisher-Price or something–something durable that I can't scratch and dent on a weekly basis. Please don't cancel the contract. Please!"

Squatting down in front of her, Malcolm rested his hands on her knees. "I would do it for you, Dani. You mean more to me than any car or...or even this business. I want to cut back on the amount of time I'm here and experience life. With you!"

"Okay. Whew!" she slouched down in relief. "Glad we got that settled.

"However..."

"Oh, no..."

"How about we work on something sturdier for you? A car we can restore together. Maybe a truck? I saw a really great '78 Dodge Lil' Red Express truck up in Virginia that I thought would be perfect for you. What do you say? You up for another road trip with me to go check it out?"

"Malcolm King, I would gladly get in the car and go anywhere with you." She stood up and kissed him. Thoroughly. When they broke apart, she gave him an impish grin. "Any chance we can take a super short road trip right now back to your place?"

Taking her by the hand, he hauled her out of her office and through the garage.

"Dad! You're on your own for the day! Dani and I have important business to take care of!"

"About damn time!" he called after them.

Laughing, they climbed into Malcolm's truck. They pulled out of the parking lot and Dani turned to him, her expression flushed and beautiful.

"In case I don't remember to say it later, this has been the greatest trip ever."

Taking her hand in his, he kissed it. "Sweetheart, this is just the beginning."

EPILOGUE

"So? How DID I DO?"

"Um "

Jumping down from the bed of the truck, Dani gave Malcolm a searing kiss before turning. "Come on. Admit it. It looks great."

"Well..." Raking a hand through his hair, Malcolm began a slow walk around the vehicle. "I thought we were going to do this together."

That had been the plan, but she had wanted to surprise him—to show him that she wasn't completely useless where the restoration of their truck was concerned. And considering it was 99.9% done, she didn't see the harm in adding the final touches. But looking at the scowl on his face, she knew it was a mistake.

With a sigh, she said, "Okay, out with it. What did I do wrong?"

He didn't speak until he had fully circled the classic truck and was standing in front of her. When his dark gaze met hers, he asked, "Did you polish that wood?"

She nodded.

"When did the decal arrive?"

"This morning and your dad was the one to do it."

Now it was his turn to nod as he looked over his shoulder at the truck. "When did the chains get here? I thought they were coming next week."

"I called the dealer and had them rush it." She shrugged. "It seemed crazy that everything was going to be done except them and it didn't cost a whole lot to expedite them, so..."

"Well, shit," he murmured, another rake through his hair.

Dani's heart sank. Here she had thought she'd done something good to surprise him and make him happy, and clearly she hadn't.

And that pissed her off.

"Look," she snapped and waited for him to face her again. "We said this was a project for us to work on *together*. We both know you did the bulk of the work so I didn't think it was a big deal for me to do these final touches."

"Dani..."

She held up her hand to stop him. "If it makes you feel any better, your father was here the entire time! Nothing is wrong! Every single thing I did, he was right here to oversee to make sure I didn't mess it up!" And when he didn't respond, she growled with frustration. "You know what? I don't care if you don't like it. I did nothing wrong." Spinning on her heel, she stalked to her office and slammed the door.

Her heart was racing and she seriously had to force herself to calm down.

Everyone knew Malcolm was a little territorial when it came to car projects, but he had really loosened up on this one because they were doing it together. They had laughed and had so much fun during the last several months with it. He taught her so much about what went into restoring a vehicle, and all the time they spent working on it really drew them closer together.

Last month, she had moved into his house and was happier than she ever thought possible. And while she knew this mood–the current one where Malcolm was being an ass–wouldn't last, it still bothered her when he got pissy like that.

She'd get over it.

And so would he.

It just sucked while they were in the middle of it.

Behind her, she heard the office door open and braced herself for whatever criticism he was about to throw her way.

Next time, she silently vowed, she'd skip the surprises.

Malcolm walked in and shut the door behind him before leaning against it. He looked miserable and her heart sank. Something was definitely up and it couldn't just be over her final touches on the truck.

So she let out a long breath and waited.

The problem with trying to surprise Dani with anything was that he never knew what to expect with her and somehow ended up being the one surprised.

It was exhausting.

There was a reason he happy to wait for those damn chains to come in–happy to put off the truck being done for another week. But she had kind of ruined his big plans and now he had to just go with it.

Something else he was having to learn to do where she was concerned.

Ever since they had officially started dating and she had moved in, Malcolm had realized just how inflexible he was. And with Dani, he certainly had to learn to be flexible. The woman hated having a schedule or anything even remotely predictable.

And he found he didn't hate it quite as much as he thought he would.

There was something to be said for spontaneity and going with the flow. He'd laughed more in the last six months and felt happier than he ever had in his life. So if his unpredictable girl upended yet another one of his carefully crafted plans, he'd just smile and cross his fingers that he could still pull this off.

She gave him that defiant look he knew so well and figured he'd better start talking.

"Let me first start by saying that the truck looks great."

Folding her arms over her chest, she said, "I know."

Unable to help himself, he chuckled. "You did a great job, Dani."

She simply continued to glare at him.

"I had planned on us finishing it together next week so I could give you this." Holding out a small bag to her, Malcolm waited for her to take it.

If there was one thing he knew about his girl, it was that she couldn't resist a gift.

"What is it?" she asked as she slowly took the white bag from his hands. "You haven't been out of town in a few weeks."

"I don't only get you things when I'm out of town."

She looked up at him briefly before her attention

returned to the bag. He held his breath as she pulled out the box. "You really didn't need to do this."

"You don't even know that this is," he teased.

Dani leaned back against her desk and took the lid off of the box. He held his breath and felt his heart sink when she looked up at him.

"You got me a toy truck?"

Clearing his throat, he took a step forward. "Not just any toy truck. See? It looks just like *our* truck. Cool, right?"

He seriously thought she'd find it endearing, but...

"I can't believe you found one that looks exactly like ours," she said, her voice holding a bit of wonder as she looked at the toy. It fit nicely in the palm of her hand. "Wait...oh! The doors open!"

"Yeah, so...I want you to know that I appreciate how you..."

"Look at this!" she gasped. "The bed of the truck moves too! And there's...wait. What is that?"

It's go time...

Dropping down onto one knee, Malcolm looked up at her. When she spotted him, her eyes went wide. "Malcolm, what...?"

Taking one of her hands in his, he gently squeezed it. "Danielle Perry, it wasn't that long ago that we were in this almost exact spot when I told you I loved you for the first time. Do you remember that day?"

"Oh, my God. What is happening?" she whispered, her beautiful eyes going wide.

"I knew that day that this was where I wanted us to go, but I knew I had to be patient." With a low laugh, he shook his head. "How's that for irony? I'm normally the one who's overly cautious and waits everything out, and yet it just about killed me to wait to do this."

Her eyes shone bright with tears as she smiled at him.

"Actually, I had planned on waiting another week," he explained and then gave her a pointed look. "The day we finished the truck. Together."

She groaned and fell into her chair–one hand in his, the other firmly grasping the toy truck. "And I ruined it," she whined.

Scooting closer, Malcolm squeezed her hand. "No, baby. You didn't. I swear." Then he paused. "Okay, I'll admit that it threw me, but...we're here and that's all that matters."

"Mal..."

"Six months," he went on. "That was six months ago. I was in love with you long before that, and I'm going to love you forever. You bring laughter and light to my days, and a whole lot of passion to my nights. You are my everything, Dani. You complete me. You make my world a better place." He paused and took the truck from her hand, and pulled out the ring that had been tucked under the tiny truck bed. Holding it up for her to see, he smiled.

And was relieved to see her smile in return.

"I love you. I love what our lives have become and I already love what they are going to be. I'm asking you, Danielle, to be my wife."

Her free hand covered her mouth and tears streamed down her cheeks as she nodded and all the nerves and anxiety he'd felt for the last several moments faded away.

"I love you so much, Malcolm," she said as he slipped the ring onto her finger.

In the blink of an eye, she was in his arms and wrapped around him, kissing him senseless. He lost his balance and fell backwards, but they held onto each other without breaking the kiss.

It seemed only fitting that something like that would happen. One kiss led to another and then there was laughter.

Malcolm knew their life together would never be boring Never be predictable.

And he couldn't wait for the next leg of their adventure.

LOOKING FOR MORE
ROADTRIPPING ANTICS?

DRIVE ME CRAZY

As far as wedding days went, Grace Mackie could say with great certainty that this one completely sucked.

And considering she was the bride, that was saying something.

Sitting alone in the bride's dressing room in the exclusive Lake Tahoe resort where her fiancé had *insisted* they have their destination wedding, she felt bored and oddly disappointed. This wasn't the wedding she had always dreamed of. As a matter of fact, it wasn't even the wedding she had planned.

Two weeks ago, Jared suggested the idea of eloping and no matter how much Grace resisted, he steamrolled ahead and now...here they were. Granted, the resort was the most luxurious she'd ever stayed at; her gown was amazing, and... even though California isn't exactly the destination that came to mind when she thought of destination weddings, it certainly didn't suck.

The downside was that they went from a big, family-filled wedding to a small and intimate event that most of her family and friends couldn't afford to attend. She had argued that point—among others—with Jared, but he had promised they'd have a big party when they got back to North Carolina. Getting married in Tahoe was a dream of his so she figured it wouldn't be so bad.

Except it was.

She was alone in this gorgeous dressing room and wished her best friend Lori or even her parents were here with her. A light knock at the door had her turning.

"Hey, Gracie! Thirty minutes until showtime! Are you ready?" The super-perky and extremely annoying wedding planner, Tilly, said with a smile as she walked through the door.

Smiling serenely, Grace replied, "Yes, thank you." Smoothing her hand down the white satin gown she was wearing, she tried to present the perfect image of the calm and serene bride-to-be.

Even though internally, she was like a squirrel in traffic.

"Great! In about twenty minutes, I'll come back and..."

"Tilly," Grace quickly interrupted before she could go any further. "If it's all right with you, we've gone over the schedule dozens of times and I'd really appreciate a few minutes to myself."

Tilly, with her severe bun and power suit, nodded. "Of course, Gracie. Anything you need," she smiled broadly and made her way back out the door, gently closing it behind her. At the sound of the soft click, Grace sagged with relief.

She hated being called Gracie. No one she knew *ever* called her Gracie. And yet for some reason, Tilly insisted on calling her that.

Catching a glimpse of herself in the full-length mirror, she should have been a happy and smiling bride. But was she? No. Instead, she was a neurotic mess who was dealing with more than your run-of-the-mill wedding jitters. She was angry, disappointed, and she knew if she didn't speak up for herself one last time, this was the way her entire marriage was going to go—with Jared making decisions she hated and then being resentful forever.

Knowing she wasn't going to breathe easy until she talked to him, Grace decided to go find him and hash this out. If it meant calling off the wedding, then so be it. It wasn't like she had any real investment in it. None of her family were here, Jared had made all the arrangements, and she had very little input into any of it.

Suddenly all the signs she should have seen were right there in front of her.

She was going to find Jared, tell him how she felt, and maybe they could look into couples counseling or something. It would be a good thing. It would help them grow closer. Looking back now, she realized this was a pattern that had gotten completely out of control. Why hadn't she noticed it sooner?

"Hindsight and all," she muttered, opening the door and stepping out into the hallway. They had toured the resort yesterday and she knew where the groom's dressing room was, so there was no need to ask for assistance from perky Tilly. At the end of the hall, she turned to the left and saw the door to Jared's room was ajar. The closer she got, Grace could hear him talking. Was Tilly giving him the thirty-minute speech too?

"You have to trust me, baby. It's all going to be okay. This is only temporary," she heard Jared saying.

Temporary? What was temporary?

"How could you do this, Jared? You said you loved me! You said we were going to be a family!"

What?!

Slowly, Grace moved closer to the door and tried to figure out who Jared was speaking to.

"We will, baby. We will," he promised. "You have to trust me, Steph. Marrying Grace will help me secure this promotion, and then six months from now, I'll divorce her and we'll be together. Just in time for the baby to be born."

Steph? *Steph?* Wait...the only Steph she knew was Jared's assistant, and he wouldn't...

"How am I supposed to come into work every day knowing you're sleeping with her every night?" Steph cried.

Grace heard Jared's soft laugh. "Baby, you need to relax. Grace and I haven't slept together for almost two months. What's a few more?"

Grace was about to barge through the door and put a stop to this, but...

"Just because she was stupid enough to fall for that whole 'wanting to make the wedding night sex better' excuse before doesn't mean she'll keep falling for it, Jared. And besides, tonight is your wedding night!"

"Don't worry," he cooed. "I'll come up with an excuse. The only woman I plan on sleeping with from now on is you."

Rage filled her, followed by a wave of nausea. How could she have been so blind? When Jared had mentioned not having sex to enhance their wedding night, it sounded kind of sexy. Hell, she had been horny all this time, and for what?

Taking several deep breaths, she told herself to calm down. Everything would be all right. She'd get through this. And then, something weird happened. She was suddenly calm—like eerily calm. It was true that Jared needed her to secure his promotion—Grace had been grooming him for the position of junior vice president of operations practically since they met! Her job as a career coach meant it was her specialty and Jared had begged her to help him move up in the company. She'd helped him change his image and his wardrobe and gave him lessons in manners and how to present himself in social situations. He was a complete doofus when she met him! And now that she transformed him, someone *else* was going to reap all the benefits of her hard work?

Well, she had news for him...he was *never* going to pull it off without her. He had definitely made great strides and his bosses were impressed, but without her there beside him, there was no way he was going to secure that promotion. His bosses weren't completely wowed by him yet and she had no intention of sticking around and helping him any longer. True, she could marry him and when he asked for a divorce, take him for everything he was worth, but that wasn't her style.

Wait, do I even have a style? She wondered.

Turning around, she made her way back toward her room and calmly walked inside and closed the door. In the corner was the small satchel that had her makeup bag, her wallet, her iPod and earbuds, her phone, and...

Before she knew it, the bag was in her hand and she was walking back out the door. The hallway was still deserted as she made her way to the rear exit and stepped outside. The sun was going down–Jared had said a sunset wedding would be romantic–and as she looked out at the lake, she had to admit the view would have been stunning.

"No time for that, dummy," she muttered, pulling her phone out of her bag and quickly pulling up the Uber app to request a ride. Saying a silent prayer that she wouldn't have to wait too long and risk someone finding her, she sagged with relief when the app showed a car was only five minutes away. Doing her best to stay out of sight, Grace hid behind some tall shrubs and prayed no one would come out and find her. Of course, a woman in a blindingly white gown didn't exactly blend into the greenery.

If they weren't so close to the ceremony time, she would have run up to their room and grabbed her luggage. Unfortunately, she didn't want to draw any attention to herself and would just have to deal with making her escape in her gown.

Staring at her phone, she willed the damn car to hurry up. The ride to the airport would take an hour, and she was hoping to get enough of a head start that should Jared try to come find her, she'd be on a plane before he could reach her.

Wishful thinking, but still...

Behind her, someone came out the back door but luckily, it was a janitor and he didn't even look in her direction. Her heart was beating a million miles an hour and when she glanced down at her phone again, she saw the car was two minutes out.

In any other circumstances, she would be pacing. Unfortunately, that wasn't an option right now and she suddenly wished she had packed a change of clothes in her satchel. If she were in jeans and sneakers, she would be trekking toward the road to meet up with the car and burning off some of this nervous energy. But no, she was stuck in this stupid, bulky gown hiding behind a shrub.

"Worst wedding day ever."

Seriously, in the history of wedding days, this one had to set some kind of new record in awfulness.

Off in the distance, Grace saw a car pulling into the resort driveway and was relieved when she realized it was her ride. Sprinting as well as she could from the bushes, she rushed to meet it and quickly jumped in.

"Are you Grace?" the driver asked.

"I am, I am," she said quickly. "Just drive. Please!" He looked at her like she was crazy but fortunately didn't hesitate to get moving. It wasn't until they were off the resort property and a few miles away that she finally felt like she could breathe. Sagging against the back seat, she immediately began searching for flights back to North Carolina. It didn't take long for her to realize she might not be leaving California or even the Lake Tahoe area tonight. Muttering a curse, she continued to search.

"Are you okay?"

She wanted to roll her eyes at that one. Did she *look* like she was okay? She was sitting in the back of a Toyota Corolla in a wedding gown and heading to the airport alone. However, she didn't think the poor guy would appreciate her sarcasm and opted to bite her tongue.

"Um...yeah," she said with a small smile. "Just...I'm not having any luck finding a flight out tonight." She scrolled the screen some more. "Where's the next closest airport?"

"That would be Sacramento. But it's two hours away in the opposite direction," he explained. He looked like he was close to her age, maybe a few years younger, and Grace remembered the app saying his name was Mark.

"Thanks, Mark. If I happen to find a flight out of Sacramento, would you be willing to drive me there?"

"Uh...I'd have to adjust the route and it's not that easy to do," he said with some hesitation. "I mean, we'd have to pull over somewhere so I could do it and..."

He prattled on a bit about all the steps it would take for him to change the route, but Grace wasn't fully paying attention. Her main priority was finding the first flight she could to get out of here. Unfortunately, it didn't take long for her to realize it wasn't going to happen. She was stuck. Her only hope was to book a flight for first thing in the morning and find a hotel as close to the airport as possible.

And pray it was next to a mall so she could buy a change of clothes.

Her phone began to ring, and Grace was surprised it had taken this long for it to start. Jared's name and picture came up and she felt sick at the sight of him. She immediately rejected the call and did a quick swipe of her screen to block his number. Not that it would stop him. All he'd have to do was grab someone else's phone and try again. Still, it was a start. Next, she turned on the do not disturb feature on her phone so she wouldn't be bothered for a little while.

"Do I need to turn around?" he asked, interrupting her thoughts.

With a weary sigh, she put the phone down. "No. We can keep going. There are no available flights tonight. I'll have to find one for the morning."

"I don't know where you're trying to go, but you could always rent a car and drive."

Again, she suppressed the urge to roll her eyes but...the idea had merit. Sure, a cross-country drive wasn't ideal, but it would give her plenty of time to clear her head. There would be no distractions and no chance of Jared–or anyone else for that matter–coming to talk her out of what she was doing.

"Mark," she said excitedly, leaning forward, "you're a genius!"

He smiled at her in the rearview mirror. "Wow. Thanks!"

"Okay, so where is the closest rental car place? I mean,

we don't have to go all the way to the airport for that, do we?"

"It might be easier, and considering it's a Saturday night, I would imagine the smaller places might be closed already. The airport car rental offices have to stay open later." He shrugged. "At least, I think they do."

Maybe he had a point, but reaching for her phone, Grace figured she could find that out for herself without any problem. "Aha! There is a car rental place just outside of Carson City and it doesn't close until eight!" She leaned forward in her seat again. "Can you get me there by eight, Mark?"

It had just started to rain, so he flipped on the windshield wipers and grinned at her. "As long as this rain stays light, we shouldn't have a problem."

Relaxing back in the seat, she felt like things might finally start going her way.

"Dude, are you all right?"

Finn Kavanagh was so busy muttering curses that he almost didn't hear the guy. Pacing back and forth in the crowded parking lot, he wasn't expecting anyone to come up and talk to him. "Yeah. Peachy, except my car is gone."

The guy looked at him in shock. He was glassy-eyed and looked no older than twenty; there was no doubt he'd used a fake ID to get into the casino, and right now was of completely no use to Finn.

"You gonna call the cops?"

Under normal circumstances he would have, but considering he knew *exactly* who had taken his car and why, it was pointless.

But he wanted to. Boy, oh boy, did he want to. Cursing again, he paced and turned and...oh, right. He still had an audience. "Uh, no. No, I'm just gonna call...a cab or something." With a forced smile, Finn walked back toward the casino as he pulled out his phone. With the help of an app, he knew he could have a ride here in less than five minutes, but he had a call to make first.

Pulling up the number, he hit send and–surprise, surprise–it went right to voicemail.

"Hey, Dave," he said through clenched teeth. "Classy move taking the car. Where the hell are you? In case you've forgotten, I'm eight hundred miles from home, and I got here in the car you currently hijacked, you son of a bitch! You need to get back here and..."

Beep!

If he didn't need the phone so damn much right now, he would have tossed it in frustration. Not that he expected his brother to answer the phone, but he also didn't expect the bastard to leave him stranded in Carson City over a petty fight.

Okay, so *maybe* pointing out how irresponsible his brother was wasn't the smartest thing to do, but who knew he'd be so willing to prove Finn right immediately?

They had decided to take this road trip together as a way of bonding. Honestly, they had never gotten along, and after trying again and again, to find Dave jobs and keep him from mooching off their parents, Finn thought the time away together would help. The idea of them being in neutral territory and away from prying eyes seemed perfect.

Clearly, he was wrong.

Now he was stranded. Dave had his car and Finn needed to get home to Atlanta so he could get back to work. Granted, he was his own boss, but the garage could only run for so long without him. Actually, it probably would be fine without him for a while, but he was responsible and the garage was his baby. He hated being away from it any longer than he had to be.

And that just filled him with rage again because thanks to his brother, he had no choice but to delay his return. Chasing Dave across the country wasn't going to be a quick and easy task, no matter how much he wished it could be.

Looking at his phone, he did a quick search for car rental places in the area. There weren't many, and the smarter thing to do would be to just go to the Tahoe airport, but that was wasting time he didn't have. The sooner he got on the road, the better chance he had of catching up with his wayward brother. Once he made a mental note of the closest place, Finn pulled up the app for Uber and ordered a car to take him there. There was no way he was flying home, even if it was the fastest way to get there. Finn had a fear of flying and just the thought of getting near an airplane was enough to make him feel a little sick. Hell, even walking back to Atlanta was more appealing to him than flying.

It started to rain and he groaned. It was the icing on the cake of the crappiest day ever. He'd already lost all the money he'd brought to gamble with and now he was going to have to pay to rent a car to get home. His luggage was in his car because he and Dave had planned on leaving tonight after dinner. As soon as they had finished eating, his brother excused himself to use the men's room and never returned.

Just thinking about it pissed Finn off more than he thought possible.

His ride pulled up just as the rain really started to come down, and he'd never been more thankful for anything in his life. Climbing into the car, he thanked the driver and immediately tried calling his brother again.

"Come on, man," he all but growled into the phone as the call went to voicemail again. "This is bullshit, Dave. It's my damn car and I can have the cops on your ass for this!" His driver eyed him suspiciously, but Finn didn't care. "Just...call me back." Again, the urge to throw his phone was great, but it would hinder more than help him.

Throwing his head back against the seat cushion, he started thinking his plan through. Maybe he should have just stayed at the casino and waited Dave out. His brother was many things, but he wasn't despicable enough that he'd strand Finn and steal his car.

Or was he?

The phone rang, and he nearly jumped out of his skin. "Dammit, Dave, where are you?"

A low chuckle was the first response. "Just drove through Fallon, but I'm considering heading south and going back to Vegas," Dave said. "Remember how cool the strip was?"

Finn mentally counted to ten before speaking. "Fallon's what...an hour from Carson City? How the hell fast are you driving?"

Laughter was the only response.

"Can you please just stay put and I'll meet you there so we can head home like we planned, okay?"

"No can do, bro. You see, you wanted to lecture me on how irresponsible I am, so you shouldn't be surprised by all of this. I mean, we all know Perfect Finn is never wrong."

If his brother were standing in front of him, Finn would strangle him. There wasn't a doubt in his mind that he'd do it. Dave could test the patience of a saint.

"Shouldn't you be trying to prove me wrong?" he asked

through clenched teeth. "I mean, that is what you normally do! Why do you feel the need to prove me right *now* of all times?"

"Ha-ha!" Dave said, laughing heartily. "I don't really care what I'm proving. All I want to do is piss you off just like you pissed me off. Doesn't feel so good, does it?"

"Dave..."

"Dammit, Finn, where do you get off passing judgment on me?"

"Right now, I think I have every right! You stole my car!"

"Technically, I'm borrowing it."

"No, you're not. You're stealing it. Borrowing it implies I gave you permission, which I did not. And how the hell did you get my keys?"

"When you went to the men's room while we were waiting for our food, I swiped them," Dave said flippantly. "So really, you have no one to blame but yourself for leaving them lying around like that."

Pinching the bridge of his nose, Finn had to wonder how he was going to get through this—or better yet, how he was going to keep himself from beating the crap out of his brother when they were both back in Atlanta.

"Dave," he began, trying to be reasonable, "you know I need to get home. Let's just agree that things got out of hand and move on, okay? Now, where are you? I'm in an Uber and can meet up with you."

The low laugh Dave gave as a response did not fill Finn with hope.

Letting out a long breath, he willed himself—again—to stay in control. "It's getting late and we're wasting time here."

"You got that right."

"It's already an almost forty-hour drive back to Atlanta, Dave. Four grueling days of driving," he added. "We weren't going to get too far tonight, but we can make up time if you just tell me where you are so I can meet you."

"Vegas."

"You're not in Vegas!" Finn yelled. "It is physically impossible for you to be in Vegas already! Now enough is enough! Do not make me call the cops! I'm serious!"

"Sorry...bad...breaking...up...later..."

"Don't hang up! Don't hang up!"

Dave hung up.

The things that flew out of Finn's mouth would make most people blush, but he didn't care. When he kicked the seat in front of him, the driver yelled, "Hey!" and that instantly snapped him out of his tantrum. He was screwed; there were no two ways about it. His brother had his car and he wasn't getting it back any time soon. The sooner he resigned himself to that fact, the better off he'd be.

So, he had to rent a car, so what? And so what if he was going to have to stop and buy himself clothes and supplies to get him through the trip? Worse things could happen. But the worst of it all was how it was going to take him longer than the planned four days. Finn believed in being smart and not overdoing things and knew driving for ten hours a day alone wouldn't be smart or safe.

Something Dave had mocked him about on their original trip.

There was a flash of lightning, and the rain was really coming down. At this point, Finn knew he would be smart to grab a car and then find a hotel and start driving first thing in the morning. With a sigh, he sat back and stared out the window until they pulled into the rental car parking lot.

"Holy crap! Did you see that?"

Finn looked out the front window toward the building and saw...wait...what was he seeing? "What the hell is that?"

The driver laughed awkwardly. "Looks like a bride—or at least, someone in a wedding gown."

And sure enough, that *was* what they were seeing. Whoever they were, they fell getting out of the car and were now in a heap of white satin on the pavement. Finn quickly climbed from the car—thanked his driver—and immediately ran over to help her.

At her side, he held out a hand to her and noticed the guy who was with her coming around to do the same. "Hey, are you okay?" Finn asked, noting the dirty gown and the curses flying out of the woman's mouth. He pulled her to her feet and held on until she was steady. The rain was pouring down on them and he did his best to guide them up onto the sidewalk and through the doors of the rental office.

She was a little breathless and pointed toward the car she'd just vacated. "My bag," she said, shaking her hand. "My bag is still in the back seat!"

"No problem," he said, hoping to calm her. "I'm sure your husband will bring it in."

Pushing him aside, she walked back out the door and slapped a hand on the trunk of the car as it was about to pull away. Finn watched with mild curiosity as she opened the back door and grabbed her bag before slamming the door shut again.

Okay, not her husband, he thought.

Because he had manners, he moved to open the door for her. "Thanks," she muttered, shaking the rain off herself—and onto him. He wanted to be mad, he seriously did, but what would be the point?

With a shrug, he walked over to the agent at the counter

and did his best to smile. "Hey...Carl," he began, reading the agent's name tag. "I would like to rent a car."

The agent smiled but it didn't quite meet his eyes. "Then you've come to the right place!" he said in a semi-flat tone. Finn would bet good money this was a repeated exchange at a car rental office.

Beside him, the bride stepped up and said the same thing to her agent–an older woman named Tammy. He looked over and gave her a small smile and wasn't surprised when she didn't give him one back. Any bride trying to rent a car while still in her wedding gown couldn't possibly be having a good day.

Finn handed over his license and credit card and waited. The only sound in the place was the typing coming from Carl and Tammy's computers. Finn looked around and saw the office was a little run-down and there weren't any cars in the parking lot.

That's when he started to worry.

The cars could be around the back, couldn't they?

"Um..."

"Oh, uh..."

Both agents spoke at the same time as they glanced nervously at each other. "Is there a problem?" he and the angry bride asked at the same time.

"Well, it looks like," Carl began.

"There seems to be," Tammy started.

"Oh, for the love of it!" angry bride snapped. "What's the problem?"

Finn had to hand it to her, she was pretty fierce. Even he stiffened up at her tone. Deciding that one of them should be respectful, he looked at the agents and smiled. "Is there a problem?" he asked.

"We only have one vehicle available," Carl said.

"Oh, well...okay." This didn't seem to be a problem for him since he got here first. "I'll take it."

"Wait, wait, wait," angry bride said, moving closer to him. "Why do you get it? We got here at the same time."

"Actually...we didn't," he corrected. "I got to the counter first, and that was after I held the door for you to come back in."

If looks could kill, he'd be a dead man for sure.

"Look, um...I know this is a bad situation," he reasoned, "but it can't be helped. It's been a really bad day and I need this car."

"Oh, really?" she asked sarcastically, motioning to her ruined gown. "And do I look like someone whose day has gone well?"

"Uh..."

"Because it hasn't!" she cried. "If we're going to get into some sort of contest over whose day was worse, believe me, buddy, I'd win!"

He was beginning to see that.

Unfortunately, he needed this car too. Maybe if he reasoned with her...

Holding out his hand, he said, "I'm Finn. Finn Kavanagh. And you are...?"

Swiping her dripping blonde hair away from her face, she eyed him cautiously. "Grace. Grace Mackie."

She didn't shake his hand.

"Look, Grace, it seems like we're both in a bad way right now. But you have to believe me when I say I *have* to have this car. You see, my brother stole my car, and I've got to get back to Atlanta and..."

"Today was supposed to be my wedding day and I found out my fiancé has been cheating on me with his assistant..."

"Okay, that does sound bad, but you see, I've got a business and..."

"And she's pregnant with his baby," she continued. "Oh, and he was planning on divorcing me in six months, so he and his baby mama could be together. He was just using me to get a promotion."

Finn's shoulders sagged even as he bowed his head.

Yeah. She had him beat.

Without a word, he motioned toward the desk and simply gave up. There had to be other rental places in town, right? And if not, he'd call for another Uber and do...something. There was a row of chairs against the wall and he walked over and sat down. He found this place by searching on his phone, so he'd just have to do it again and hope he'd find another one.

Scrolling...scrolling...scrolling...

The rustling of wet satin had him looking up. Grace was two feet away and still staring at him hostilely. "Problem?" he asked, letting his own annoyance come through.

"Listen, it seems to me we've both had a crappy day and...well...I'm heading across country too. So, if you want to share the car..."

He was instantly on his feet. "Seriously?" Then he got suspicious. "Why? Why would you even offer? You know nothing about me, and for that matter, I know nothing about you."

She rolled her eyes. "Both Carl and Tammy mentioned there not being another rental place nearby. The closest one is about twenty miles from here and is closed for the day. Your only other option is the airport and..."

"I'm not flying!" he snapped and immediately regretted his reaction. "I mean...I don't really like flying so..."

"No, I mean there are car rental places there you can

try, but it's still a bit of a drive to get there too." She paused and fidgeted, and Finn figured her dress had to be a bit of a pain to move around in—even more so now that it was wet. "Nothing today has gone as planned and I'm not looking forward to driving across the country alone."

"I get that, but still...how do you know you can trust me?"

"Honestly? I don't. But Carl and Tammy have your license and would know I was leaving with you, so if anything happened to me, you'd be the guy everyone would go after." Then she paused, and her gaze narrowed. "Is there a reason I shouldn't trust you?"

"What? I mean, no! There's no reason," he stammered.

"Tell me about yourself," she said before turning to the curious agents. "You guys listen in on this too. You're witnesses."

"Witnesses? That's just..."

"I'm just trying to be practical, Quinn," she said.

"It's Finn," he corrected and then cleared his throat. "I'm Finn Kavanagh and I'm from Atlanta, Georgia. I was born and raised in East Islip, New York, and moved to Atlanta when I was eighteen. I'm thirty years old and I own my own auto repair shop, Kavanagh's. You can look it up online. We have a website and a Facebook page," he added.

"Tammy, can you check on that please?" Grace called over her shoulder, not breaking eye contact with Finn.

Finn glanced toward the counter and saw both agents typing and nodding, and when Grace looked over at them, they both gave her a thumbs up.

It was ridiculous for him to sag with relief, but he almost did.

"Anything else?" she asked. "What about your family? You married?"

"No."

"Girlfriend?"

"No."

"Boyfriend?"

"No!" he shouted a little too defensively.

"Any siblings other than the car-stealing brother?"

He shook his head. "Nope. Just Dave."

"Why'd he steal your car?"

"It's a long story..."

And for the first time since he'd met her, Grace gave a small smile. "Good thing we've got a long drive ahead of us and you can tell me all about it."

This is crazy, he thought. There was no way he was going to drive cross-country with a complete stranger. He didn't do things like this! He was fairly practical and cautious, and this had disaster written all over it.

Grace walked back over to the counter and Finn followed. "My turn," he said.

"For what?"

"Tell me about yourself."

She leaned against the counter and looked at him with mild annoyance. "Why? It seems to me I'm the one at greater risk here."

He gave her a bland look, crossed his arms over his chest, and waited.

With a sigh, she said, "Fine. Grace Mackie, career coach, age twenty-eight. Recently ran out on my wedding. I was engaged to the cheating jackass for six months and we dated for a year before that. I have two brothers and one sister, who are all happily married to non-cheating jackasses."

"A career coach?"

She nodded. "I too have a website and Facebook page,"

she turned to Tammy. "Executive Career Services by Grace out of Raleigh, North Carolina. You can Google it." They waited all of two minutes before Carl and Tammy gave another thumbs up.

"Looks like we're both who we say we are," Grace said, her smile growing a little.

"Looks that way," he agreed. "The only problem is you're going to North Carolina and I'm going to Atlanta. How's that going to work?"

She considered him for a moment. "I'd be more than willing to go to Atlanta with you and fly home from there. Unlike you, I'm not in a rush. The longer this trip takes, the better."

Finn didn't take that as a particularly good sign, but he wasn't going to question it right now. Hell, if she wanted to camp out in Atlanta once they got there, who was he to argue?

Still, he wasn't so sure this was going to work.

"Are you willing to split the driving?" he asked.

Grace let out a mirthless laugh. "Dude, I was planning on doing *all* the driving a few minutes ago. If there were more than one car here, I *would* be doing all the driving. So the fact that now I don't have to? Um...yeah. I'd say I'd be willing to split it."

Okay, so she was snarky, but he was going to blame it on the fact that she'd had a bad day.

For now.

"We each pay our own way, right? We'll split the cost of gas, but other than that, you're on your own for the things you need."

She rolled her eyes before shaking her head. "Do you even hear yourself? We just met, for crying out loud! Why would I expect you to pay for anything for me?" Then she took a menacing step toward him. "Are you always this uptight and ridiculous?"

"Ridiculous?" he cried, mildly annoyed. "How am I being ridiculous?"

"Um...excuse me," Tammy called out, interrupting them. "But we're getting ready to close so...are you going to take the vehicle? We can put both names on the rental agreement if you'd like, or we can leave it in Miss Mackie's name."

For a moment, neither spoke. Then Grace seemed to relax a bit. She studied him for a long moment before speaking. "So what do you say, Finn Kavanagh? Are we taking this road trip together?" She held out her hand to him, and for a moment, Finn questioned his own sanity for even considering this. Unfortunately, she was his only hope right now.

And before he could question himself any further, Finn met her hand and shook it. "Looks like it, Grace Mackie."

DRIVE ME CRAZY is available everywhere now!
https://www.chasing-romance.com/drive-me-crazy

ABOUT SAMANTHA CHASE

Samantha Chase is a *New York Times* and *USA Today* bestseller of contemporary romance that's hotter than sweet, sweeter than hot. She released her debut novel in 2011 and currently has more than sixty titles under her belt – including *THE CHRISTMAS COTTAGE* which was a Hallmark Christmas movie in 2017! When she's not working on a new story, she spends her time reading romances, playing way too many games of Solitaire on Facebook, wearing a tiara while playing with her sassy pug Maylene...oh, and spending time with her husband of 29 years and their two sons in Wake Forest, North Carolina.

Where to Find Me:

Website:
www.chasing-romance.com
Facebook:
www.facebook.com/SamanthaChaseFanClub
Instagram:
https://www.instagram.com/samanthachaseromance/
Twitter:
https://twitter.com/SamanthaChase3
Reader Group:
https://www.facebook.com/groups/1034673493228089/

Sign up for my mailing list and get exclusive content and chances to win members-only prizes!
https://www.chasing-romance.com/newsletter

ALSO BY SAMANTHA CHASE

The Enchanted Bridal Series:

The Wedding Season

Friday Night Brides

The Bridal Squad

Glam Squad & Groomsmen

The Magnolia Sound Series

Sunkissed Days

Remind Me

A Girl Like You

In Case You Didn't Know

All the Befores

And Then One Day

The RoadTripping Series:

Drive Me Crazy

Wrong Turn

Test Drive

Head Over Wheels

The Montgomery Brothers Series:

Wait for Me

Trust in Me

Stay with Me

More of Me

Return to You

Meant for You

I'll Be There

Until There Was Us

Suddenly Mine

A Dash of Christmas

The Shaughnessy Brothers Series:

Made for Us

Love Walks In

Always My Girl

This is Our Song

Sky Full of Stars

Holiday Spice

Tangled Up in You

Band on the Run Series:

One More Kiss

One More Promise

One More Moment

The Christmas Cottage Series:

The Christmas Cottage

Ever After

Silver Bell Falls Series:

Christmas in Silver Bell Falls

Christmas On Pointe

A Very Married Christmas

A Christmas Rescue

Christmas Inn Love

Life, Love & Babies Series:

The Baby Arrangement

Baby, Be Mine

Baby, I'm Yours

Preston's Mill Series:

Roommating

Speed Dating

Complicating

The Protectors Series:

Protecting His Best Friend's Sister

Protecting the Enemy

Protecting the Girl Next Door

Protecting the Movie Star

7 Brides for 7 Soldiers

Ford

7 Brides for 7 Blackthornes

Logan

Standalone Novels

Jordan's Return

Catering to the CEO

In the Eye of the Storm

A Touch of Heaven

Moonlight in Winter Park

Waiting for Midnight

Mistletoe Between Friends

Snowflake Inn

Wildest Dreams (currently unavailable)

Going My Way (currently unavailable)

Going to Be Yours (currently unavailable)

Seeking Forever (currently unavailable)

CPSIA information can be obtained
at www.ICGtesting.com
Printed in the USA
LVHW090153050521
686553LV00010B/33

9 798666 621363